EAST OF ANYWHERE

SIX UNLIKELY POETS ON A JOURNEY TO HEAL

RICK THORPE

Black Rose Writing | Texas

ISBN: 978-1-68433-255-7
PUBLISHED BY BLACK ROSE WRITING
www.blackrosewriting.com

Printed in the United States of America
Suggested Retail Price (SRP) $19.95

East of Anywhere is printed in Chaparral Pro

Author of plenty of other things you've probably
never read or even heard about.

Acclaim and random comments for Rick Thorpe's
EAST OF ANYWHERE

"[One] of the [best] books I've ever read... and I've read several, believe me."
-Tim Brink, Delaware

"Of all the books written this decade... this is one of them."
-Charles Tereck, Cincinnati

"[I] couldn't put it down... fast enough."
-Jon Dumbauld, Texas

"Rain showers in the Northeast today..."
-Sonny Flowers, local weatherman

"[We] found [ourselves] crying... when he asked us to review it."
-Tony Beccaccio and Jeff Ginsberg, Cathedral City, Calif.

"Your prescription is ready for pickup..."
-Pharmacy voicemail

"Every once in a while you find *that* book... that's been overdue at the library."
-Gary Baker, New Jersey

"[A] dazzling foray into... something... I'm not sure what. It's bound to sell
dozens."
-Walter Balcar, Jacksonville

"[A] few pages in you'll find yourself... on the second or third page."
-John Hibner, Paris

"I didn't read it... I assumed it sucked."
My brother, St. Paul

"Please stop following me..."
-Total stranger, Columbus

This work is dedicated to my father, Richard D. Thorpe, who taught his children the importance of art, the written word, and humor.
You are greatly missed.

East of Anywhere

MATTY CAHILL

... ran out of the journalism building his brown curls bouncing. He realized he had forgotten his favorite ball cap so he quickly turned, ran up the steps three at a time to retrieve it. The act was going to make him late to his next class but it didn't matter, the hat is priceless. His dad had bought that hat for him on his tenth birthday at a Pirates game. He came from a big family and money was tight, for his dad to take him to a game meant the world to Matty. He loved the Pirates but he loved having a day a whole day with his dad even more.

It was an extremely windy day so he held onto his hat as he hustled to his ethics class. There were more students enrolled in the course than there were seats, but as the semester went on people skipped the class freeing up some room. Matty found only one available seat in the back row, he plopped down in it, pulled his laptop out of his backpack and settled in for his last class of the day.

Matty never missed a class, although he was tempted to on many occasions. He had promised his mom he would work hard and earn a degree- a first for his family. She had wanted him to stay closer to home and attend a community college, but finally relented when Matty convinced her he needed a school with a strong writing program.

The professor was organizing her notes when a kid hobbled in on crutches. Matty did not know him well but they had lived in the same dorm their freshman year and had often played together in pickup basketball games. He was pretty sure his name was Walter. The guy was from Cleveland and Matty always gave him a hard time about the Browns. Matty waved him to the back row when he saw the distressed look on his face at the full classroom.

"It's Walt, right?"

"Matty?"

"Yep." Matty smiled and gave him a fist bump. "Here take my seat, buddy. Pretty hard to takes notes while standing on one foot for an hour."

"Are you sure, man? Thanks, I really appreciate it. I tried to get here early, but I just haven't gotten the hang of walking with these damn things yet."

Matty got up, moved his backpack and sat in the deep windowsill behind the now empty seat. Walt dropped in the chair while Matty took his crutches for him and leaned them against the wall.

"Bust up your ankle playing hoops?"

"Naw, I slipped in the cafeteria."

"A grape?"

"Worse... a deviled egg."

"They are evil bastards... thus the name."

Walt let out a laugh just as the professor was getting ready to start. He turned and whispered, "Thanks for the seat, buddy... but the Steelers still suck."

Matty smiled and powered on his laptop from his perch on the windowsill.

·　　·　　·　　·　　·

On the way back to his room his thoughts were of food. Lunch had consisted of an apple and half of a stale granola bar. It was too early for dinner but he knew he couldn't write the paper he had due on an empty stomach. Although on a strict budget he was really getting tired of ramen noodles. Matty didn't like fast food so he stopped into the Broad Street Diner.

Matty took a booth by the window and looked at the menu. He checked his wallet to determine what he could afford. It looked like he would be getting the grilled cheese and tomato soup, the cheapest items on the menu. It wasn't much but a heck of a lot better than ramen. He set down the menu and smiled at the elderly waitress who was slowly making her way towards him. Her dyed auburn hair was curled up in a bun, her name tag said 'Nora'. In spite of her weary appearance, she smiled in return.

"What can I get for you, honey?"

"I will have the grilled cheese on wheat and a cup of tomato soup, please."

"Anything to drink?"

"Hot tea, please."

With an extremely shaky hand she wrote down his order. The look of concentration and frustration on her face said a lot. Matty looked away to not embarrass her. Ten minutes later she returned with his order. The cup of soup was only half full. Matty didn't complain, just smiled.

"Thank you so much. It looks great, Nora."

"Sorry about the soup, honey. I was afraid if I filled it to the top I would spill it. I'll bring you another half cup when you are ready."

"To be honest with you, I'm not very hungry, half a cup is perfect. Thanks again."

Matty wolfed down his meal, using the last bite of his sandwich to sop up the remains of the soup. The waitress stopped by the table to collect his dishes and drop off his bill. Matty got out his wallet and had just enough cash on hand to pay the bill. He felt bad leaving just a one-dollar tip, his mom was a waitress, he knew it was tough work. He took a pen out of his book bag and wrote a note on the bill. Matty left the money and the tip on the table and made his way to the restroom before he left. In the meantime, the waitress picked up the bill, money, and the tip. She strained to read the note Matty had written on the dollar.

'Dear Nora,
Sorry for the skimpy tip, it was all I had. Next time I will do better. I wanted you to know you are the best waitress I have ever had. Keep up the good work! Because of your fine service I will return.
Sincerely,
Matty Cahill'

Matty returned from the restroom and headed for the door, still a little hungry. Right as he was ready to exit. The waitress called after him.

"Wait, son... you forgot the rest of your soup." The waitress was holding an extremely large takeout container of tomato soup, thankfully, with a lid.

"Wow, thank you!" Matty said with surprise.

"You're welcome," she said while handing him the container. She dapped at her eye with a napkin then winked at him.

Matty left the diner out onto the windy street. He turned, looked through the glass window and waved to Nora. She smiled and returned the wave before waiting on an impatient customer.

Instead of looking through the window, Matty now looked *at* the window. A flyer caught his eye and had him intrigued. The wind was making the paper whip around. He thought to himself that it should have been taped on the inside of the window instead of on the outside. Matty set his soup down on the sidewalk and held the flyer down so he could read it. With his free hand he took out his phone and took a picture of it. The moment he took his hand off the flyer it ripped free and flew into the air heading skyward. Matty watched it flutter away as he headed home.

He smiled to himself thinking about the brief encounter with Nora, for a moment it damped his ever-present sadness. His father had always preached to him, 'If you want happiness and contentment in life, put other peoples' needs ahead of your own'. At one time Matty only practiced that when it was convenient, like holding a door for someone. The past year or so he had made a strong effort to put it into practice. At times it was very difficult and he would slip up now and then or people would take advantage of his thoughtfulness. Regardless, he made a vow to put others first.

Matty read the flier again from his phone, nodded when he finished then stuffed the phone in his back pocket. He pulled his hat snuggly down on his head and thought about the paper he was about to write.

WAYNE BUBULSKI

... sat wedged in his cubicle at work. A small cubicle and a rotund man are a bad combination. He felt like a cork in a bottle. Wayne kept glancing at his watch. Only ten o'clock, he was starving and lunchtime was two hours away. He hoped the cafeteria had his favorite today, pot stickers. Thank goodness it was Friday, doughnut day. Wayne thought about getting another one... or two. He knew his co-workers would look at him and; A. roll their eyes, B. smirk, C. talk about him behind his wide back, or D. some sort of combination of A, B, and C. 'Screw them', he thought, he would go get more but he didn't want to walk to the conference room to get any more. He looked at his empty paper plate, the only thing left were some sprinkles that had fallen off the five doughnuts he had eaten earlier. Wayne rolled the plate into a tube, checked to see if anyone was watching, then poured the remaining sprinkles into his mouth. Hmmm, sprinkles.

He looked at the pictures pinned up to the walls of his cubicle. He sometimes pretended the faces looking at him were spectators and he was a cage fighter, knocking out his arch enemy with his patented backhand slap. In truth, the pictures were fake. Not fake people, (they were models that came in picture frames) they were fake family and friends. He did not get along with his family and had few friends.

Only one picture was real, a picture of a person from his past. He kept meaning to take that one down but he just couldn't bring himself to do it. His current love interest, Jerri, refused to give him one. Many excuses were given why, "I don't have any that I like", or "Wait till I drop a little weight first." Wayne became weary of the excuses so he finally quit asking.

•   •   •   •   •

At long last lunchtime finally came. Wayne labored his way to the cafeteria and got his beloved pot stickers, plus a ham and cheese sub, a large taco salad, two pieces of coconut cream pie. Ironically, he washed it all down with a gigantic Diet Coke. He usually sat with James McDowell, the only co-worker he could tolerate. James was the polar opposite of Wayne in many respects, he was thin, friendly, and outgoing. How James tolerated Wayne was a mystery to their co-workers. James is, by nature, an empathetic person. Perhaps he saw a side of Wayne that others did not see or bother to look for due to Wayne's aloofness and arrogant bearing.

James noticed Wayne eyeing the peanuts on his tray.

"Want these?" James said pointing to the package.

"No thank you."

"Just got a case of *peanuts* envy, do you?"

"Hardy har har," Wayne said dryly.

"Want to hit the Gym after work?" James asked through a mouthful of carrot.

"I don't know, James."

"Come on, dude! It'll make you feel good."

"I suppose, my date for tonight was canceled...again."

"Do you want to pump iron or hit the treadmills?"

"How about a little of each?" Wayne said after some thought. "Let's get there right away before all the muscle heads get there."

"Sounds good. We'll get you ripped in no time."

"The only thing that will ever be ripped on me is the backside of my britches."

James let out a hearty laugh but stopped quickly when he saw that Wayne was straight-faced.

"Alright, man, I'll see you at the gym." James stood and picked up his tray, he started to leave but then he hesitated for a second.

"Yes?" Wayne said seeing the uncomfortable look on James' face.

"Uh, Wayne," James said then paused, looking for the right tactful words. "Could you try to cover up yourself in the locker room?"

"Doesn't one need to be naked in order to take a shower?" Wayne asked with irritation.

"Well, sure..." again, James struggled to find the right words, "but do you need to strut around like Mick Jagger in there?"

"Is it not obvious that I can't wrap myself in a towel? They're way too small and bringing in a beach towel is out of the question. If the gym members are uncomfortable with nudity, then they can just-"

"No, No," James interrupted, fearing what Wayne was about to say. "You are right, man... why would people be bothered by a very large, wet, pasty-white fellow walking around in a very small locker room? Forget I mentioned it."

"I already have," Wayne said with a heavy sigh.

•   •   •   •   •

That afternoon during break time, Wayne took the elevator to the top floor of the high rise. When he was feeling morose, he would go out on the roof for some much-needed peace. But only if the pollen count was low. The melancholy he was experiencing was happening more and more often. He knew in his heart that his devotion to food was due to a longing in his heart. Wayne felt like the U2 song *I Still Haven't Found What I'm Looking For*. Perhaps he wouldn't know what he was really longing for until he came upon it.

Wayne would sometimes walk to the edge and look down... like he was doing now. He wondered if he were to 'accidentally' fall from this building would his co-workers notice that he was gone? Would there be any impact besides the impact he made on the pavement? He imagined they would hear and feel the explosion he would make. This fat man would rival the Fat Man that was dropped on Nagasaki. Broad Street would never be the same. The cleanup would take at least a week. He smiled at the morbid thought.

He backed away from the edge and looked up at the clouds. Clouds always lifted his mood. Today the sky was as blue as... as blue as... heck, no simile could do it justice. Believe me, it was blue... a great contrast to the billowy, alabaster clouds that were cruising by. He spread his mammoth arms, closed his eyes, and lifted his head towards the clouds. He looked like an inspirational poster... for Weight Watchers. He was about to open his eyes when a piece of litter smacked against his face. Wayne grabbed it before it flew off. He could not believe he was hit by a fluttering flying flyer. As he read it he thought it must have been a serendipitous gift from the clouds. He held it tight as to not lose it as he made his way back to the elevator.

LEON JIMENEZ

... sat in the teacher's lounge at Central High School with his head in his hands. Planning period is the best time to get some work done, but also for peace and quiet. He desperately needs both. He had a rough day and wanted to be alone for a bit. The quiet solitude broken when he heard the door open and the familiar whistling of his good friend Stanley Watts. Stan's hair was thinning so he had recently started shaving his head. Stan wore baggy sweaters or loose shirts every school day to hide his weight. You could always count on Stan to put a smile on your face. Watts and Leon had taught together for over twenty years and were pretty tight, constantly messing with each other. They were two of the six minority teachers working at Central.

"What's up brother, Leon?" Stan said while mussing up Leon's curly hair.

"Not much, Stan. What's shaking... besides your man boobs? Math world treating you right?"

"Numbers are numbers, they don't change much," Stan said with a grin. "You like the new look?"

"Your noggin looks like a Milk Dud."

"That joke is gettin' old, buddy, you need to come up with new material. You sure you're okay? You look like my favorite Miles Davis album... *Kind of Blue*."

"I got accused of being a racist by a student, can you believe that?"

"By a white kid? I get that at least once a semester if someone doesn't get the grade they want," Stan said running his hand over his slick head.

"Nah, an Asian kid. You know Annie Chow?"

"Yeah, had her last year. Kinda homely lookin', kids call her Dog Chow behind her back. Unfortunately, it's true, but very mean. I put a stop to that immediately. She's a nice kid, what happened?"

"She got a good score on a tough quiz so I drew a little smiley face on it. She said I made slanted eyes on the face to insult her. I told her all my smiley faces look the same, I make them in about half a second."

"She wasn't convinced?"

"Nope, went and complained to Henderson."

"You shittin' me? Annie went to the principal over a damn smiley face?"

"Yep."

"And I bet that fat assed, toupee wearin', skirt chasin' fool was no help to you at all."

"Hell no, called me into his office, coffee breath all up in my grill, shows me the correct way to draw a smiley face."

"Come on, man."

"I ain't lyin'! The man got a compass out of his desk and made a round circle and gave it dot eyes and a smile."

"I know you, man. You messed with him, didn't ya? Played along?"

"You know it! I said, 'That's a great smiley face, Mr. Henderson, but won't my bald, round-headed, white kids be offended?'"

"Let me guess, you're straight-faced as hell, so he don't know you dickin' with him?"

"Right, you know the man...but it gets better."

"Bring it."

"Henderson is noddin' his head in agreement, So I said, 'How about when I draw a smiley face, I make it look like that particular student *intentionally*? Make 'em feel special and unique.' I take the pencil off his desk and shade the face dark and for hair I draw a box fade on top, and then I say, 'Now, that covers Shawn Sully.' I draw a new smiley face with long hair and mutton chops and say, 'That covers Christian Thomas, how about one with a beard for Zeke Williams.' Henderson gets it now, sees the sarcasm, and he's gettin' pissed. But of course I don't stop."

"Of course."

"So I throw in, 'Let's draw a goth kid with dark eyeliner and a nose piercing... no, that won't work, smiley faces don't have noses... shucks!'"

"You said 'shucks' 'cause his country ass is always sayin' that."

"Yep. I started laughin' and he pointed towards the door."

"Brother, you know he will retaliate. Your Dominican behind is gonna get parking lot duty breakin' up fights between the homies and the rednecks."

"It was worth it. I laughed the whole way back up here... but then I got bummed out..."

"'Cause of Henderson?"

"Hell no, because I got to thinking about how a student has lost faith in me."

"You're a good teacher, Leon. And a good man, Annie will figure that out."

"Thanks, Stan. I appreciate your friendship, man. You've always had my back."

"And you, mine… now let's not get all mushy. How are the kids holding up?"

"They have their good days and bad days… just like me."

"It takes time… look I gotta get to period three. Call or text if you need anything."

"Thanks, Stan. I will. And I like the new look, you resemble a short Charles Barkley."

"Thanks… I think."

•   •   •   •   •

Leon made it through the rest of the day without any other mishaps. Annie Chow had even stopped by to apologize. She said she was overly sensitive due to having some issues with her friends. She got weepy as she talked to him, told him he was her favorite teacher. He almost hugged her but knew that might not be too smart in this day and age. He shook her hand and accepted the apology. He wondered if Stan had said something to her.

On his way out of school he checked his office mailbox. He found a folded piece of paper and a note to call a parent, Ralph Diaz. His shoulders slumped and he let out a sigh, kicking himself for checking his mailbox. Leon decided to call Mr. Diaz now and get it over with. The day before they had had a pretty heated conversation. He used the secretary's phone and dialed the number. He turned his back to the secretary and walked out as far as the phone cord would stretch, knowing that the secretary would try to listen to the conversation.

"Hello."

"Hi, Mr. Diaz. This is Leon Jimenez returning your call."

"Yeah, about our conversation yesterday…"

"Hey, I apologize for that. I was way out of line to tell you how to parent your son."

"Well… I was mad as hell at you… but the truth is I was embarrassed. You were right."

"You had every right to be mad, I overstepped my bounds."

"I needed the wakeup call. You said I needed to spend more time with

Frankie. I got to thinkin' about it, had me a long talk with the boy."

"That's great. I hope it was productive. He's a great kid, just a little lost right now."

"Yeah, he is a great kid; thank you. He got a lot off his chest. I'll spare you the details but the bottom line is I've been putting my business ahead of my son, and that's not cool."

"I only said what I said because I know firsthand how fast time goes with our kids. Before you know it they're gone."

"Well, like I said, I apologize for gettin' so mad and also for the language I used. It takes a lot of balls...er, guts to tell it like it is. I respect that. Most people tell you what they think you want to hear."

"I appreciate that Mr. Diaz."

"Please call me Ralph."

"Okay, Ralph... have a great evening and call me again if I can help you with anything. Oh, one more thing. You own the Jiffy Lube on Broad Street, right?"

"That's right. Worked my way up the ladder, took out a loan and bought the franchise rights five years ago. I recently went in with a friend and bought another one on High Street. Want a free oil change?"

"No thanks, that's very nice of you. I was in there the other day for service and my daughter's sunglasses disappeared."

"Man, I am so sorry. We have had a lot of that lately. I'll look into it and if my manager can't get to the bottom of it, I'll replace the sunglasses."

"No, don't worry about it. They were gaudy and cheap but I told her I'd ask about them, and I thought you ought to know."

"Thanks, I appreciate it. Again, I'm sorry about that, Mr. Jimenez. Goodbye and I'll be in touch."

•　　　•　　　•　　　•　　　•

Leon hung up the phone and breathed a sigh of relief. He had dodged a bullet. For years he had been biting his tongue with parents and fellow teachers. It was one thing, of many, that bothered him about the education system. Parents could tell you exactly how they felt with little or no repercussions, tear you a new ass if they were so inclined. Could a teacher do the same? Hell no. 'Hey Mr. Smith, this is Mr. Jimenez calling to tell you your parenting skills suck. Furthermore, if you don't stop drinking and beating your wife, you're gonna have a kid just like you. Thanks, and have a wonderful day.' Tell a parent that and you'd be on the street looking for new work. For the past couple of weeks, he had been brutally honest with people and he knew he had better cool it, he had kids at home he needed to support.

He stuck his hand in his pocket and took out a guitar pick. He rubbed the pick tenderly between his fingers then gently put it back in his pocket. He then opened the folded piece of paper that had also been in his mailbox. It looked like a flyer of some sort, still had the staples in the corners. He glanced over it.

"I know this from you, Stan," he said out loud.

The secretary gave him a quizzical look. He wadded the paper into a ball and took the posture for shooting his patented fade-away three-pointer towards the wastebasket.

"No thanks, Milk Dud."

Another, even more quizzical look. He bent his knees and was about to shoot when he paused, as if frozen and slowly put the ball of paper in his battered leather briefcase and headed out the door.

ED BAKER

... leaned against the four board fence. It was close to noon and late in the day to be letting the horses out to graze. It had rained hard for the past few days and he wanted to let the pastures dry out a little more before putting the horses out. Ruben and Shaq were the first two horses to be led out today. Due to the rain the horses had been cooped up in their stalls for two days. Ed knew they would be ramped up.

He normally took the horses out two at a time, today he knew better. Ruben was the first to go out, it took a firm grip on the lead rope to keep him from taking off. Ed wanted Ruben to run around by himself first. Shaq was older and Ed didn't want him to try to match Ruben's spunk. He knew even though Ruben had settled down he would act up again when another horse came out. Sure enough, as soon as Shaq was released they both bucked and kicked out. Ed prayed they didn't accidentally kick one another. Obviously, a kick from a horse can inflict damage, but a kick from a horse wearing shoes, which they both had on, could be serious. His next concern was that one of them might throw a shoe due to the muddy conditions.

The two horses started to sprint in tandem. Manes blown back, muscles rippling, tails trailing like flags. Globs of mud and grass sprayed behind them. Ed pulled off his old ball cap and ran his hand through hair rapidly turning gray. He replaced his cap, stretched and grinned. Days like this are what he lived for.

When the horses finally settled down to graze, Ed examined a splinter he had in the palm of his left hand. He took his old Buck lock blade out of his pocket and worked on the splinter. Not a day went by that he did not use that knife for something. Ed always kept the Buck 110 clean, sharp and well oiled, it had belonged to his dad and he was glad it was handed down to him. He hoped someday to give the knife to his own son. Ed's hands were thick with calluses, he rarely wore gloves, the splinter was embedded at a shallow angle and came out easily.

While the horses were eating their morning grain and hay, Ed had fixed fence boards that were loose or broken, thus the splinter. Some of the horses like to lean against the fence and rub when they had an itch. One horse, Buster, like to scratch his large hind end on the fence, moving his feet up and down in place like he was doing the cha-cha. It always made Ed smile until he heard the creaking and popping of boards.

Once all the horses were out, Ed stripped the stalls of their sawdust bedding and opened the bottom of the Dutch doors so the stall floors could dry out. He noticed his supply of sawdust was running low. He'd have to give his friend Harold a call soon and have him bring a load from the sawmill. The water buckets looked like they all could use a good scrubbing so he did that as well. When he was finished he thought about sweeping out the barn, instead he opened the barn doors at both ends and hoped the wind would do the job for him. Ed was satisfied with his work in the barn so he jumped on the tractor that pulled his manure spreader and headed towards his backwoods to empty it.

· · · · ·

Back at the house, Ed stopped on the porch, took off his boots, and went in to grab a bite to eat and to pay some bills. The house was quiet, the only sound coming from the ticking of an ancient grandfather clock and the rhythmic drip in the deep kitchen sink. He loved the old farmhouse but he never could get accustomed to the quiet during the day. At one time the house was filled with family noises; screen doors creaking and slamming, one-sided telephone conversations, muffled music from an upstairs bedroom, off-key humming coming from the kitchen. Noises that, at the time, wore on and irritated him. When he came home from a stressful shift in a police patrol car he wanted some quiet. Like a lot of people in his situation, he now longed for that noise.

Ed made himself a sandwich, cut himself some tomato slices on a plate, and took it out to the back screened-in porch. This was a different kind of quiet, a quiet he could handle and enjoy. He finished his late lunch, leaned back in his rocking chair and closed his eyes. He took pleasure in watching birds but what he really loved was listening to them, it gave him great peace. His wife had hung a wind chime off the back porch many years ago. It was pleasant sounding, and she really liked it, but now that she was gone he would take it down in early spring and not put it back up till winter. He wanted to hear his birds without the accompaniment of metal tubes. Ed took a deep breath and sighed. As beautiful as his life was, deep seeded nagging thoughts kept him from truly being satisfied... He shot straight out of his chair.

The shotgun blast brought him back to a violent time. This was not a dream for once, but from a nearby field. His friend and neighbor, Lawrence, had been after a brazen coyote for some time now. Gunshots did not bother him when he was expecting them, he had grown up hunting and as a policeman had spent many hours at a shooting range. It took several minutes for him to calm down and get his heart rate back to normal. Ed had made a lot of growth, but in spite of that; there was a dark place that would occasionally rise up to haunt him.

Two quick beeps from the postal truck told him he had mail. Tim, his mailman, always gave him a signal when he had a letter or bill. If Tim didn't hit the horn, then Ed knew there had been nothing for him that day, saving him a trip to the box.

Ed walked through the house, put his plate in the sink, slipped his boots back on and walked the gravel lane to his rusty green mailbox. He pulled from the box a *Western Horseman* magazine and a letter from his brother. Art Baker worked for the fire department and lived about thirty minutes from Ed's farm. Ed wondered why Art didn't just call him or swing by. He smiled when he saw a smudge of red pottery clay on the backside of the envelope. Ed opened the envelope and pulled out a flyer. There was no note or explanation. After reading the flyer, Ed shook his head and laughed. "Just like Arthur, always there to help someone out," he said to himself out loud.

He stuffed the flyer and the envelope into the magazine, rolled it up and put it in his back pocket. At that moment a motorcycle came rumbling down St. Rt. 40. From a distance it looked like a vintage Harley or Indian motorcycle. As it got closer, Ed could see it was an Indian. The enormous rider raised his hand as he cruised by. Ed raised his hand in return, watched the bike disappear down the road towards the city. He watched for a bit, then turned and walked the dusty gravel drive back to the house.

Ishmael Hatmaker

... sat in the cluttered office of the Broad Street Jiffy Lube waiting for his boss, Richard Small. Through the grimy, fly speckled office window, Ishmael watched Small being backed up against a rack of Quaker State oil, forty-weight, by a busty Latino woman in very tight clothing. Ishmael could not hear what they were saying, but Small had his hands up in surrender, the woman seemed to be riled up about something. She was stomping her foot while poking Small in the chest with a finger, with the other hand she pointed at Ishmael.

'Well I do believe that little Senorita is sweet on me,' Ishmael thought as he wiped a dirty shop rag across an even dirtier forehead. He then stood up, put a thumb to his ear and his pinky towards his mouth, imitating a phone. "Call me," he mouthed towards the Mexican bombshell, punctuated with an exaggerated wink and several cocky bobs of his head.

Ishmael hung up his imaginary phone to admire his reflection in the office window. His flaming red hair was wild and unruly. He started to run his hair through his mane when he realized his hands were covered with grease and grime. 'Ah, why mess with perfection,' he thought. He was checking out his bird-like profile when a quart of Pennzoil, thirty-weight, smashed against the office window. Ishmael about jumped out of his pale skin. After he regained his composure, he grinned and watched a honey-colored ooze slowly glide its way down the glass, pulling with it several dead flies.

Through the ooze, Ish could see the woman stomping off. Richard Small was chasing after her with a fat fist full of coupons. The woman stopped, grabbed the coupons and threw them right in Small's face. Ish let out a snort when he saw that a coupon had stuck to Small's sweaty forehead.

Small made his way back to the office in a huff. Ish quickly sat back down on a tattered couch. Small open the door, stepped in and slowly closed the door behind him. He paused for a moment, eyes looking toward the floor, composing himself. He took a deep breath and exhaled slowly.

"Ishmael... since you have been working here I have had five complaints about you... *and* you have been late four times. The owner, Mr. Diaz, is pissed."

"Only five complaints and four lates? That ain't so bad."

"You've only been working here a week."

"Well, when ya puts it that way..."

"Did you really say, 'Nice pair of melons ya got there, Senorita.'"

"She had two cantaloupes sittin' on the passenger's seat!"

"But your eyes weren't on the cantaloupes!"

"Look, Mr. Small, Dick... if I may."

"You may not."

"Okay, *Richard*, I was just tryin' ta be friendly."

"What you call '*friendly*' everyone else calls harassment. Have you ever heard of the *Me Too Movement*?"

"Nope."

"Figures... I'm afraid I'm going to have to let you go."

"But I gots the most edjacation on this here entire crew!"

"You *have* the most education."

"That's what I said!"

"Look, Ish, six years of high school is nothing to boast about. Sorry, but it's time for you to leave."

"Whatya gonna tell my sister?"

"We are no longer dating... so I won't be telling her anything."

"Was it the food poisonin'?"

"That and the fact she looks a great deal like *you*. Look, you can keep the uniform, but I'm going to have to remove the Jiffy Lube tag."

With stubby little fingers, Small tried to tear off the tag. After numerous attempts, he was only able to rip off the J in Jiffy.

"That will have to do, damned thing is sewed on pretty good."

Small tossed the J into a trash can overflowing with fast food wrappers. Ish stretched, yawned and gave Small a friendly pat on the shoulder. His former boss looked at the greasy handprint Ish had left on his white dress shirt. Small gritted his teeth and pointed towards the door.

"Well boss man, it was nice workin' for ya. Any chance I could get that little Senorita's phone number?"

"Please leave now."

"Okay, okay, keep your dirty shirt on. I'll just get my lunch and be movin' on." Ish said as he opened the old white refrigerator in the office and took out a sack lunch.

"Ish, that looks a lot like my lunch."

"All brown bags looks a like, Dick."

"Get out!"

Ish let out a chuckle and headed out the office door. He walked through the work area and shouted to the three Hispanic men who were busy changing oil on three separate cars. "Later on my little beaner friends!"

All three looked up but did not say a word. In unison like a drill team, they all gave Ish the middle finger. Ish chuckled again and walked through the garage door into the noonday sun. Squinting, he looked around while contemplating how he was going to spend the rest of his day. It dawned on him that he had recently 'acquired' a pair of sunglasses from the passenger's seat of the last car he serviced. He pulled them out of his back pocket and examined them. They had gigantic lenses covered with fake jewels, obviously a woman's pair. They were a little bent from him sitting on them, he straightened them out and slipped them on with a smirk.

•   •   •   •   •

Ish walked six blocks down Broad Street and stepped into a corner market.

"Hadji, my man, how ya doin'?"

A thin, dark store clerk leaned against the counter and rolled his sleepy eyes when Ish walked in and let out an exasperated sigh.

"You have been coming to my store for three years now. You know my name is *Rehan*, not *Hadji*."

"Sorry, but ya looks like that little brown feller on the cartoon, Johnny Quest."

"Never seen it, but it sounds like something you would enjoy, juvenile, racist and offensive. What can I get for you today, the usual, *Miss*, a Pabst tall boy and a bag of pork rinds?"

"*Miss*? What the hell..." Ish then realized he was wearing women's sunglasses. "Very funny, just the Pabst today, got me a sack lunch." Ish held up the brown bag and waved it in the air.

The clerk retrieved the beer from the cooler and set it on the counter. "Two dollars."

"Here ya go, chief," Ish threw two crumpled bills on the counter. "Where's that old woman that normally works the early shift? She your Mama?"

Rehan balled up his fists, leaned forward and said through gritted teeth, "That *old* woman is my wife!"

"Whoa! Your *wife*? Was that one of them *arranged* marriages? If it was, ya got the short end of that deal. If I was you..."

"Get out!"

Ish threw both hands up in the air in surrender, picked up his beer off the counter and sauntered out the door. He walked a block or two and sat down on a bus stop bench to eat his lunch. He reached inside the bag and pulled out a sandwich wrapped in foil. As soon as he opened the foil his head snapped back from an overwhelming stench. Ish peeled back the soggy white bread and found the source.

"You gotta be kiddin'! He said out loud. "Who in the hell eats tuna fish and garlic? That damn boss man done screwed me over again."

Ish was hungry so he shrugged his shoulders and took a big bite washing it down with a hit of beer.

"Not too bad," he said with a grin, "and I won't have to worry 'bout no werewolf attacks."

Ish took another bite of the sandwich when a small brown stray came up to him wagging his tail. The mutt was dirty and so thin you could count his ribs.

"Hey little fella," Ish said while rubbing the dog's head, "ya wants some of my sandwich?"

Ish tore off a hunk and gave it to his new friend who gobbled it down quickly. Ish started to tear off a piece for himself, when the dog snatched the sandwich out of his hand and scampered down an alley.

"Damn, I can't buy me a conversation today... or a friend"

A second later an old red firebird screeched to a stop in front of him. 'Hell,' he thought, 'careful what ya wish for.' With some effort the firebird window was rolled down, and a large round shaved head popped out. The face broke into a big grin with several teeth missing.

"What up, cuz?"

"Hey, Jasper."

"I gotta be honest with ya, cousin Ish. With your red hair, big beak, and them fancy shades, ya looks like the lovechild of Woody Woodpecker and Elton John."

"And you looks like the offspring of a pumpkin and a jack o lantern."

"How redundant."

"I know, it's a gift,"

Jasper shook his head in disbelief, "Ya heard from your folks?"

"Nah, they bought a cap for the pickup truck and took off without sayin' a word."

"Dude, that was five years ago!"

"I know, I'm startin' ta get worried... but then again, they never cared too much for me."

"That's a damn shame, you bein' such a devoted son and all."

"I hear ya," Ish said shaking his head. "If ya recall, I had that high fever when I was a kid. Lasted almost a week. They said it messed up my brain. We started drifting apart after that."

"Well, I know one thing... you act just like your daddy."

"For real?"

Jasper saw a look of pain on Ish's face and decided to change the subject.

"Why ain't ya workin'? Get canned again?"

"Nah, I'm lookin' inta other opportunities."

"Sure," Jasper said with a laugh. "Hey, you seen that new nurse at the free clinic?"

"Nope, ain't been there in years."

"Oh yeah! They ask ya not to come back after that pee sample mishap."

"All a misunderstandin'."

"I'm sure they've forgotten all about that by now. I'm tellin' ya gotta check out that new nurse."

"A real looker, huh?"

"Would I lie to ya, cuz?"

"Hell yes ya would," Ish said with a smirk. "Hey, you ain't seen Alice around anywheres has ya?"

"Nope, not hide nor hair... but if I does, I'll take her on over to my place for safe keepin'."

Jasper tried to keep a straight face but he grinned and let out a loud cackle. He hit the gas on the firebird and left Ish standing in a plume of white smoke.

"Very funny ya pumpkin headed bastard!" Ish shouted at Jasper as he peeled away. He thought about throwing the can of Pabst at the car but it was out of range and he was thirsty.

•   •   •   •   •

Ish wandered down the street lonely and bored. 'I should look for another job,' he thought. 'Nah, maybe tomorrow.' He tossed his empty beer can towards a dumpster but missed, gave a slight shrug and kept walking. A grin came across his face and he headed toward the free clinic.

There were several people waiting in line ahead of him. A fight broke out in the waiting area. The people in line all moved over to see what the commotion was. When they did so, Ish slipped to the front of the line. No one was at the front desk so he took the opportunity to once again admire his reflection in the glass. He smoothed back his hair and tucked in his dirty work shirt before pounding on the glass with the palm of his hand.

Out of the corner of his eye Ish saw a nurse in robin egg blue scrubs coming out from a back room. Although the person had delicate features, Ish was shocked to see that the nurse was a small man, he frowned.

"Patience, patience," the nurse said and returned the frown.

His wavy dark hair was gelled and had frosted tips. Ish noticed he had multiple earrings, a small diamond stud in his nose, and a hoop in one eyebrow. The nurse saw the greasy mark Ish had left on the glass and let out a sigh. He grabbed a bottle of Windex, a roll of paper towels and vigorously wiped the glass clean.

"How can we help you today?" the nurse asked with a hint of irritation.

"I ain't sick or nothin', it's just I'm from the neighborhood and I was just thinkin' I could use me a checkup," Ish said while looking at the man's name tag, it read *Ramone*.

The nurse handed Ish a clipboard with a piece of paper on top.

"Please fill this out the best you can."

"Sure, sure, *Ray Moan*," Ish said while looking around the clinic for another nurse. "If you're too busy, I can have another nurse check me out."

"It's *Ramone*, one word not two. I'm busy, but not too busy to help you. You see I'm new here and I need the practice."

'New nurse. That damn Jasper pulled a fast one on me', Ish thought.

"Well okay, but can we make it quick? I got places ta go."

"Absolutely," the nurse said looking Ish up and down. "Let me make sure I have plenty of rubber gloves. I'll be right back."

Ish began to fill out the information sheet as best he could. He made up an address in case the nurse fella had ideas about making a home visit. The nurse returned just as Ish finished up.

"So Mr..... Hatmaker, I see you live on *Straight* Street, is that correct?

"Yep."

"You said you're from the neighborhood, so am I by the way, but I've never heard of Straight Street."

"It's a road I'm sure you've never been down," Ish said, struggling without success to suppress a grin.

The nurse closed his eyes and took a deep, calming breath before he spoke.

"Okay, Mr. Hatmaker, head back to examination room number three. Once there, please disrobe, sit on the table and cover yourself with a large sanitary paper. You will find a dispenser on the wall. Dr. Campbell will be in to see you shortly."

"You got it, chief."

Five minutes later Ramone knocked on the exam room door.

"Come on in, Doc!" Ish hollered from behind the door.

The nurse opened the door and found Ish sitting on the exam table wearing nothing but a large paper hat folded to resemble the tall three-tiered crown worn by the Pope.

"What the hell, Ramone? I thought ya said a doctor was comin' in!"

"She asked me to do your blood work first," Ramone said, turning his head to avoid looking at the naked Pontiff. "The paper was to cover your *privates* not your head."

"Ya shoulda been more clear about that!" Ish said, removing the hat and using it to cover up his lap, then adding, "I bet ya weren't clear on purpose, wantin' ta see me in my birthday suit!"

"Mr. Hatfield, I am a professional," Ramone said through gritted teeth.

"Now please give me a finger."

"I'd like ta give ya a finger alright," Ish mumbled while extending his left index finger.

It took Ramone several alcohol wipes and hard scrubbing to get the finger clean.

"You're going to feel a little prick."

"I betcha say that ta all your boyfriends," Ish said with a snort, "Now I... OUCH! Why'd ya stick me so hard!"

"I bet you say that to all of your boyfriends." Ramone said calmly as he drew the blood sample into a small tube. "I'll send the doctor in after we run your blood work."

As Ramone left he turned down the thermostat to fifty degrees.

•   •   •   •   •

Ten minutes later, Dr. Campbell came in. She was short, squatty with an athletic build and short blond hair, her glasses at the tip of her nose. She had a pensive look on her face as she read over a report.

"Hello Mr. Hatmaker," she said with a cold tone. "Nice tattoo," she added with sarcasm. "I've got some serious news for you."

"Bra..bra..brake it to me gen... gen...gently, Doc," Ish stammered through chattering teeth.

"You appear to be myopic and also suffering from a raging case of homophobia," the doctor said completely straight-faced.

"Is th...th...there a c...cure?"

"You'll need a change of heart."

"A tra..transplant?"

"Not a new one just a change. You'll start by apologizing to Ramone."

"I ain't ap.. ap..apologizing ta that weir...weirdo!"

"Fine," the doctor said while slipping on a rubber glove. "No apology, no pants."

She took the pants off the hook on the wall with a tongue depressor, leaving only a shirt, apparently he had not been wearing underwear. The doctor then calmly walked out.

•   •   •   •   •

Thirty minutes later, Ish was waiting on the front steps of the clinic for Jasper to pick him up. He had used the clinic phone, without permission, to call him. While he was waiting he read the various fliers that were taped to the front glass of the clinic. One seemed to intrigue him. He peeled the flyer off the glass, folded it up and tucked it into his shirt pocket just as Jasper came rumbling up. Ish crinkled down the steps towards the firebird. He had made a pair of underwear out of the large sanitary paper from the exam room. It looked as if he was wearing a giant diaper.

Jasper let out a hoot, "Now ya look like a cross between Woody Woodpecker and Gandhi!"

Ish climbed in and slammed the car door, "Go ta hell Jasper."

DANIEL L'OURS

... rumbled into town on an old Indian motorcycle. This was not a planned destination, he usually never had one in mind. Daniel, running low on cash, needed to find work. This being his usual modus operandi, work for a month or two, save up some money and move on. He had been on the bike for several weeks now, stopping to nap under a tree or a cheap motel when the weather was poor.

It would be a cliché to say he enjoyed the freedom of the open road. There was some truth to that, but what really gave him pleasure was seeing and learning new things. Daniel would spend time studying things, absorbing them, whether they be majestic or mundane. He had always been that way. Relationships were few for Daniel, even polite conversation being rare. Even though he was a good-looking man with short black hair and piercing blue eyes, people had a tendency to shy away from him. Being reserved by nature, was part of the explanation, but the real reason people kept their distance? Daniel L'Ours was an enormous and intimidating hulk of a human being.

    •   •   •   •   •

Daniel entered the city limits from the west heading east on St. Rt. 40. Interstate 70 would have been faster but he always traveled on the nation's backroads or *Blue Highways,* as writer William Least Heat-Moon called them, to see the most interesting part of the country. St. Rt. 40 became West Broad Street as Daniel got into the city. The buildings became cleaner and taller the deeper he traveled into the city's downtown. He passed several hospitals, law firms, investment companies and plenty other businesses he had no use for. A slight smile appeared on his face as he entered an area of town overflowing with art galleries. He downshifted the Indian so he could get a better look. One particular piece of art displayed in a window caught his eye, a large painting of the Flatiron Building. It was in a classy shop, *The Gallery Harris.* Daniel was familiar with the artist and he made a mental note to stop in once he got settled.

Once the galleries, cafes, and bookshops ended, the bars, tattoo parlors, and liquor stores began. This is where Daniel would find work. He didn't mind manual labor, especially construction work, he actually enjoyed it. But he found it a better fit for him to work at night so he could have the day free for going to libraries, museums and parks. He spied a *Help Wanted* sign in the window of a bar, *Benito's Billiards and Beer*. Intrigued by the name, Daniel slowed down and pulled his bike over. He killed the engine, took a worn leather saddle bag off the bike and threw it over his shoulder.

Upon reaching the litter-strewn sidewalk, Daniel noticed a drunk passed out lying in front of a bench. His brothers would have called the guy a piss-bum and kept walking. Daniel knelt down and checked on the guy assuming he might have rolled off the bench. His assumption was correct; the side of the man's head was bleeding slightly. Not too big of a bump, no need for stitches and already starting to clot. Daniel took a water bottle from his saddlebag and gently poured water on the wound to rinse out the dirt and grit. He then took a clean bandanna out of his back pocket and wrapped it around the guy's head. Daniel held his breath (his brothers would have been right, he smelled like stale urine) and gently as he could, lifted the man and placed him back on the bench. He then took out a black t-shirt, folded it into a square and laid it under the man's head. Under the man's arm, Daniel tucked a small wrapped loaf of French bread which would have been his lunch. He thought for a moment, pulled a money clip out of his front pocket, peeled off a couple of bills and shoved them deep them into the guy's shirt pocket. He hoped the guy would use the money for food but realized he probably wouldn't. If anyone had been watching Daniel they would have seen that the whole time his facial expression remained neutral, revealing nothing. He showed no look of concern, pity, revulsion, or sorrow. But he did pat the man gently on the shoulder as he walked away, a small act that spoke volumes.

•   •   •   •   •

He found the door to Benito'propped open. Daniel entered the doorway and stopped before going any further to give his eyes time to adjust to the darkness. From a distance he heard the swish of a broom stop in mid-swish.

"Who in the hell shut the door!" a gravelly voice called out. Daniel's height and width blocked the sunlight from entering the bar, a human eclipse. He stepped sideways to let the light back in.

"I'm sorry, sir," Daniel said quietly in a voice as deep as a well.

"Sweet Jesus," the voice answered with a trace of fear after seeing Daniel. "Are you a bill collector?"

"No, sir. Just looking for work."

"Thank God," the voice whispered.

Daniels eyes adjusted, he could see a small old man with a broom. The old man held the broom in his left hand while the right was clutching his chest. He tentatively hobbled towards Daniel. He was stooped over, bald on top with long reddish gray hair on the sides. He wore round spectacles, a white dress shirt, and worn red house slippers. He let go of his chest and extended his hand.

"Franklin Silverstein," the old man said. "Ya gave me a bit of a start."

He tried to give Daniel a firm shake but could not wrap his fingers around the mammoth mit. Daniel knew better than to squeeze his hand. It's difficult to land a job if you turn someone's carpal bones into powder.

"Daniel L'Ours, nice to meet you Mr. Silverstein."

"L'Ours... that's kinda ironic to have a name like that bein' as big as you are."

"You speak French?"

"My mother was from Quebec. You probably think it's ironic that my name is Franklin when I look like Ben Franklin."

"Never entered my mind," Daniel said with a slight smile.

"Sure it did, the look is intentional. I sometimes fly a kite just to see the reaction. Lookin' for work are ya? How do ya look in a low cut waitress outfit?"

Daniel smiled again, "Probably as good as you do."

Silverstein let out a snort, "Now that's funny. I need a door man to check ID's and keep peace."

"A bouncer."

"Yep."

"I've had some experience with that. I don't have a résumé or references."

"Your size is your résumé and those scars on your fists are your references," Silverstein said with a sly grin, but then he paused and rubbed the white bristles on his chin. "Those scars concern me a little bit. I want altercations *prevented* not started."

Daniel stuck out his massive hands and displayed them, something he never did. He thought long before he spoke. "I understand your concern, but as you can see these scars are old and starting to fade. They are... from my youth."

"Who would be stupid enough to fight you?"

"My three brothers. We had a makeshift boxing ring in our backyard."

"Tough were they?"

"My brother Paul would fry bacon... naked."

"Now that's a badass. Play any ball, did ya? Wrestle?"

"Polo."

"Ha! On what, a Clydesdale? I think I'm going to hire you based on your humor more than your size."

Silverstein brought his arm up to slap Daniel on the back to seal the deal, but he realized the giant was so tall that the friendly pat would land on Daniel's ass instead of his back. He didn't want to be accused of sexual harassment... or die. Instead, he reached out and shook Daniel's hand again. Daniel smiled, nodded his head and remembered not to squeeze the elderly hand.

"May I ask, who is Benito? A former owner?

"There is no Benito. I made that up because it sounds better."

"Alliteration."

"Sure, whatever. I tell people Benito is a silent partner. A rumor started that this is a mafia owned bar."

"And logically you didn't kill the rumor."

"I started the rumor," Silverstein said with a laugh.

The old man looked around Daniel and saw the old Indian motorcycle parked out front. "That your bike?"

"Yep."

Silverstein walked outside to get a better look. His mouth dropped open. "Is that a 'forty-eight?

"Yep."

"Not many of this style known to exist."

"Hop on."

The old man handed Daniel his broom and climbed on the bike. His tobacco stained teeth were beaming.

"This thing is worth a fortune. Where did you find this gem?"

"It was my brother's. It took him over seven years to restore it," Daniel said with a tone of reverence and respect.

"Let me guess, you'll never sell'er."

"Never," he whispered.

•   •   •   •   •

That night Daniel was stretched out on a mattress in a small apartment above the bar. He threw the mattress on the floor, as was his habit, for fear he would crush the bed frame. The apartment was cramped, hot and stuffy. Daniel had opened a window that overlooked an alley. Silverstein offered it to him free of charge in exchange for keeping an eye on the bar at night. Apparently there had been quite a few break-ins in the neighborhood this month and the old man was getting nervous. Silverstein had scheduled to have an alarm system put in, but he got to thinking that Daniel might be better and cheaper than an alarm.

Sleeping, or rather, not sleeping had always been an issue for Daniel for the past several years. He had a difficult time shutting down his mind. Once he was able to settle his mind, a ghost from his past would whisper to him and he would struggle with sleep for other reasons. Tired of lying there he got up and went down to the bar, wearing only jeans. He did not go there to drink, but to exercise. He found a couple of empty beer kegs and moved them in various directions to warm up his muscles. Once he thought he was ready for it, he picked up two full beer kegs. He guessed them to weigh 150 pounds each, perhaps a little more. He did the same rotation of exercises and movements with the full kegs. He curled them, pushed them over his head, squatted, lunged, rowed and anything he could think of. After forty-five minutes he was spent, his muscles were gorged with blood. A big man appearing even bigger.

He found a bottle of tonic water behind the bar and poured himself a tall glass. He finished the water and went to the sink to wash the glass when he heard a noise, like a door slowly creaking open, in the back pool room. He set down the glass and walked quietly towards the noise. He stopped and listened outside the doorway. He definitely heard whispering. Daniel reached inside the room and flicked on the light switch. Two disheveled looking men both shouted with a start when they saw Daniel, shirtless and sweaty standing over them. One guy had a pool stick in his hand and out of fear swung at Daniel. Daniel caught and grabbed the stick just as it was about to crash into the side of his head. He snapped the pool stick like a dry twig with a flick of his thumb, the broken half clattered to the floor. The intruder still held on to the other half. Daniel lifted his arm straight up and the guy now dangled in the air like a piñata. He was about to bring his free hand into the guy's ribs. When a voice called out, "Daniel, stop!"

It was Silverstein, he came walking in the open back door. "I hired these bums," he said sheepishly.

Daniel let go of the broken pool stick and the fellow on the other end fell three feet to the floor below in a heap. "Please explain, boss," Daniel said calmly.

"I wanted to see how alert you were, so I paid three unemployed hillbillies ten bucks a piece to break in and steal some a bottle of cheap Tequila I had sittin' out open on the bar. If they came back with it, they could keep it. Been wantin' to get rid of that bottle forever."

"Ya coulda got us done killed!" the man on the floor whimpered, still rattled.

"Not killed, just in the hospital for a few days," Daniel said evenly.

"Would a done ya good," Sliverstein said with a smirk. "Mighta dried ya out."

"Very funny, old man."

Silverstein saw the second hired intruder hiding behind a pool table, shaking like a leaf.

"Where's the third guy?" Silverstein asked.

"Right befores we was fixin' to come in, he says, 'I think I sees Alice.' He then takes off runnin', I think he was chicken... he even looks like one."

"That hilljack owes me ten bucks," Silverstein said with frustration.

"the problem is... they didn't break in, they just opened the door. How was I supposed to hear that?"

36

"I know, I know... I thought about that... I opened the door for them with my key. I didn't want to have to pay to fix a busted door, I was already out thirty bucks as it was. I'm not sure these nitwits could have figured out how to break-in anyway."

Daniel shook his head and smiled, 'This is going to be an interesting job,' he thought.

•   •   •   •   •

After Silverstein and the two men left, Daniel picked up the broken pool stick and threw it in the trash. He found a French bread wrapper behind the pool table where the second intruder was hiding. He laughed out loud.

The next morning Daniel woke up feeling blue. He didn't have to put his finger on the cause, he wore the cause like a shroud. He knew one way to shake it off; walk to a library, a gallery, or a museum, perhaps all three. Daniel looked over his motorcycle like a cowboy would inspect his favorite horse. Silverstein had let him keep it in a back storage room, guessing its value both monetary and in sentiment. He pulled off the tarp he had draped over it and gave it a pat, which was his ritual, and covered it back up. Daniel went out the front door of the bar and locked it behind him. He saw a flyer on the outside bar window that caught his attention, he stopped to read it. He took a small notebook and pencil out of his pocket and jotted down some information before he went exploring. A modern Gulliver on the east side of a new Lilliput.

A QUICK SNAPSHOT INTO THE FUTURE...

A faded green Ford pickup truck sat parked outside the ER. I checked out the truck bed and saw what appeared to be a lot of loose hay. On the tailgate sat a half-used roll of duct tape. Seeing the hay led to the assumption that this truck belonged to Ed, therefore the right hospital. I'd rather the men not know that they were being checked on, so I looked around my car for a discrete disguise. The objective was not to spy on the men, namely Ishmael, but to check on them... without them knowing. So, I guess I was spying.

I flipped up the collar of my jacket, and put on my sunglasses, in spite of the fact that my dashboard read seventy degrees and nine o'clock at night. I found my son's little league baseball cap on the floor of my car, slapped it across my thigh a few times to get the dust off, and put it on. It fit like a yarmulke; I probably resembled a Mossad dropout. Nevertheless, it was the best I could do. I was a sixth-grade teacher, not Ethan Hunt from *Mission Impossible*.

Upon walking into the ER waiting room, I spied Ed stretched out in a chair, his long legs straight out, worn boots crossed one another. His hands were behind his head, his weathered cap pulled down over his face. Being a retired cop, I guessed he didn't stress over the events of tonight.

The veteran nurse at the front desk, I would guess, had seen about everything you could imagine... until now. Daniel, the giant, dressed in all black, as always, stood before her blocking most of the light like he had a tendency to do. To his right slumped Ishmael. What a sight. Ish being held at the elbow, like a child, in Daniel's enormous right paw. The back of his scrawny frame and his wild red hair were covered with random bits of hay. Around his forehead an eight-pound bag of convenience store ice, held in place with duct tape. The weight of the ice being too much for Ish's skinny neck, caused his head to bend forward. Water from the melted ice rolled down his large beak of a nose and dripped to the counter below. Daniel noticed this and backed Ish up a step.

I continued to watch from the corner of my eye while pretending to make a choice from a vending machine. The nurse asked Ish questions and typed them into a laptop. Ish answered in a shout, perhaps because he could not see how close he was to her. Ed never stirred from his nap. From around a corner a security guard came walking at a brisk pace, with a furrowed brow. When he saw Daniel he stopped on a dime, turned around and headed the way he came, pretending he had an urgent call on his radio.

The nurse, perhaps assuming Ish was hard of hearing, started to speak louder.

"Occupation?" she asked.

Ish hesitated as if thinking. This a rarity. "I'm a... I'm a pizza de-"

"He's a poet," Daniel interrupted with a straight face.

"You're a poet? Like Robert Frost?" The nurse asked with evident sarcasm.

"No, miss, I'd be a more like William Carlos Williams," Ish declared, head held high, in spite of the ice bag. "He was a doctor ya know? Hell, he mighta even worked at this here hospital."

"I think we better get you looked at," the nurse said, a concerned look on her face.

Daniel let out a laugh. Another rarity. The booming laugh startled Ed, and he started to stir. This being a cue for me to leave. Slipping out the door, I glanced to my left just in time to see Wayne waddling his great bulk down a side hallway. He also had an icepack, though hospital issued. Wayne held it against his right hand. I only saw him for an instant, but I swear he was smiling...

INTRODUCTION

(If you are curious or confused, read on.)

I will make this introduction as brief as I can for two reasons. One; I don't want to lose anyone reading this, and two; Dad would have wanted this to be concise. So here goes.

My father was a therapist and a university professor. He employed different methods and techniques over the years to help thousands of patients heal and recover from, or manage, various mental health issues. His success rate high, and well respected in his field. I don't believe any of the methods he used were too controversial or radical; he being rather conservative by nature. For most of his career, Dad used journaling with his patients. Of all the methods he used, journaling being the foundation. One class he taught at the university; *Cognitive Behavioral Therapy: Identifying disordered thought through journaling*. That's a mouthful. My brother said it sounded like a snooze fest... I'm sure that's true.

Dad had always been intrigued by the use of art as therapy. One of his close friends, a fellow therapist, swore by it. My mother is an artist, also teaching at the university, so Dad would witness firsthand how the act of painting or drawing could bring about so much pleasure and satisfaction. Unfortunately, he felt like he was too close to the end of his career to be trained in art therapy. One day while looking through my bookshelf he was struck with an idea he could not get out of his head.

He found one of my favorite poetry books, *Reflections on a Gift of Watermelon Pickle... and other modern verse*. The editors of the book were able to capture the mood of many of the poems with black and white photographs. It's a book for young people, but it works for adults as well. Dad became enamored with it as much as I when I first found it.

"Have you ever tried this with your students?" Dad asked.

"You bet. Look at this book." I showed him a copy of the book *I Wanna Take Me a Picture: Teaching Writing and Photography to Children*.

"Does it work? Do the kids like it?"

"They love it. It works because the writing and photography complement and feed each other. It's also a great way for me to collaborate with the art teacher."

His face lit up. "What if I had a group of patients write poetry, and when possible, take a photograph to match the mood, tone, or message they were trying to convey? A photograph would not work with every poem, and you wouldn't want to force it or for it to be a distraction. But with many poems, especially ones written by novices, I think it could work. A purist would disagree, but screw them."

"Sounds interesting," I replied. "Has anyone tried something like that before?"

"I'm not sure, but I don't think so. This could be a chance for me to experiment with art therapy, and in a roundabout way, the poetry will substitute for the journaling that I typically use."

"Poetry and photography are both forms of artistic expression."

"Absolutely. Now I need to figure out how to make this work."

I'm not sure when I had seen him more excited about something. He had a long and successful career, but retirement loomed ahead, and I think he thought this might be a great way to really end on a high note. Two weeks after that conversation, he called me. His enthusiasm had not waned.

"I think I have figured out how to put this poetry slash photography therapy into action."

"Shoot."

"I want to start with a small group of let's say half a dozen men, who are all dealing with loss in their lives of some sort."

"I'm with you so far, but why just men?"

"Not just men, but I'll start with a group of men and then try a group of women. I have found people are more likely to express themselves if they are in the company of others of the same gender. Think about it, when you were in a writing or speech class, did you feel self-conscious in front of the females?"

"I felt self-conscious in front of everyone. I felt self-conscious in an empty room, but I see your point."

"Thank you."

"But there might be some men who would feel more comfortable with men *and* women in the group. What will you do if you have someone apply from the LGBTQ community? You aren't going to discriminate are you?"

"I'm not going to discriminate. You know me better than that. By all means, I *want* diversity. Look, are you going to pick this idea apart or listen?"

"Okay, okay, I'm sorry. How are you going to go about recruiting this group of men?"

"This is the tricky part. I know this is going to sound really out of the norm, but I think I'm going to advertise in the local papers and post flyers around the city."

"No offense Dad, but what type of person is going to respond to an ad or a flyer for therapy?"

"A person who is curious and willing to try something different in order to heal."

His tone told me that he was growing weary of my numerous attempts to play the role of the devil's advocate.

"I'm sorry, Dad, and again I don't mean to offend, but aren't you afraid you are going to be bombarded with responses from a bunch of nuts?"

"This isn't very professional of me, but for over the past forty years, I've dealt with more *nuts* than Planters!"

"Again, I apologize; I need to trust that you know what you are doing."

"Thanks, I appreciate that... Now you are really going to love what I tell you next."

"Hit me."

"I'm going to pay them to participate."

"*Pay* them? Why? Look, I don't have a clue on how to run a mental health business, but doesn't the average therapist *charge* their patients?"

"To explain this in a *nut*shell...This is an experimental form of therapy as far as I know, and I want to have the right to record each session and use it as a case study and possibly publish the results... if they are positive. If I am *paying* the subjects, they will be more likely to agree to my terms as part of the contract they will sign. They will, of course, also be expected to show up to every session, if possible, and to produce work in order to be paid."

"That makes sense. Where is the money coming from? Are you going to apply for a grant from the university or some other source?"

"I thought about that, but applying for grants and waiting for an answer can take forever. I'm seventy years old; if I'm going to do this thing I want to get started right away… so I'm going to finance this myself."

"Mom okay with that?"

"Yes, yes, I checked with her, of course, to see how she felt about it. She said we had plenty of money socked away for retirement, and I'm not going to retire from the university yet, just from private practice. I had set aside about ten thousand dollars for some home improvements… but now you and your brother will be doing those."

"Great… Bill will love hearing about that."

"You're a teacher; you've got nothing better to do this summer."

"Aren't you worried some guys will sign up just for the money?"

"I've considered that, but people will need to contact me if they are interested, and then I'll interview anyone whom I feel is a potential candidate. People try to bullshit me on a daily basis; I'm pretty good at seeing through it."

"Sounds like you have thought this through."

"To be honest with you, it's all I have thought about since I saw those books at your place. Oh, and I almost forgot to add, and this is big, the university has agreed to grant the participants three college credit hours."

"For free? That will be *huge* incentive for some people."

"I hope so. The university is also going to let me use a classroom and a projector one night a week. It helps to have friends in very high places. But honestly, the university is anticipating some recognition, and rightly so, if this is published and is successful."

•　　　•　　　•　　　•　　　•

The next step for Dad was to recruit potential candidates. He wanted a diverse group, if possible. It really depended on who applied. To increase his odds of diversity, especially in terms of age, he knew he had to reach out further than just the university; thus the idea to advertise in papers and post flyers. He was not a fan of social media, so that was not going to be an option.

Next, the problem of how to word the ads and flyers. This was an unusual request, '*Looking for men dealing with grief or loss, who would be willing to write poetry and take photographs.*' This might not seem like an odd request in New

York or San Francisco, but this being the Midwest. I had a vision of a long line outside of my dad's office that resembled open auditions for *The Village People*. After some fine-tuning, he was able to word an ad that sounded unusual but somewhat logical. It was also decided that the participants could choose, after completion of the workshop, either the 3 credit hours *or* a thousand dollars, not both. (Of course, my brother and I were hoping the men would choose the three credit hours with the hope that he and I would get out of doing the home renovations).

Ads were placed in several local newspapers. On a sunny Saturday, Dad distributed several hundred flyers. He accomplished this with the help of his two sons, and a handful of his university students (students whom I assume were in desperate need of extra credit). We divided the city as best we could and posted on telephone poles, message boards, and shop windows (only a few shop owners agreed to this). The shop owners in the rougher neighborhoods were more receptive to let us post flyers; the more affluent sections of the city frequently turned us down. It was tiring work, but we did it and Dad was pleased, and that made it worth it. I found out later one of the college students paid some kid ten bucks to post his flyers. I was disappointed... that I did not think of it.

Dad received about two hundred inquiries of which about half were legitimate. He narrowed the pool down to twenty men and interviewed them in his office. It was very difficult for him to narrow it down to six. Several of the men, he admitted were a risk to select. Most of them had very little writing experience and practically none of them had very strong photography skills. His greatest fear, being that some of them would not produce quality work, but he thought it worth the risk because their presence might make the group more interesting. He made it clear to all the men that he had selected that if they did not make a strong effort they would be dropped from the program and receive no compensation. Asking for trouble? Probably, but it was his course/experiment and I knew he could handle any bumps in the road. Although a caring and compassionate man, he could be a tough old bastard when he needed to be.

Dad had a few things he needed to take care of before the class began. One, he had to secure the classroom, projector, and the video recording equipment promised. Two, he had to line up an instructor from the art department to give a good lesson and tips on how to take a halfway decent black and white photo. Third, he put together a packet for each man containing an outline of the course, a schedule, and a contract to sign. After he took care of those three things... he died. You read that right; two weeks before the course was to begin, my father had a massive heart attack and died.

•   •   •   •   •

With the help of my brother, I laid my father to rest. We then did the best we could to comfort our mother and help her with all the financial and legal documents, all while still grieving ourselves. Understandably, the course was the last thing on our minds. Three days before the start of the course my brother Bill brought it up.

"What are you going to do about Dad's course?"

"Cancel it I guess. And why is it up to me?"

"For several reasons; one, you have the same name, two, Dad always liked you best, and three, you still live in town. You can't cancel the course. That would have killed him... if the heart attack hadn't gotten him first."

"And who is going to *run* the therapy group?"

"Well *you* of course... You're a teacher."

"I teach sixth grade, Bill! These are men! Besides, I'm not qualified as a therapist or a counselor."

"I didn't say it would be easy, but you would be more of a facilitator than an instructor or counselor. Just steer them in the right direction and it will all work out."

"That's easy for you to say, you'll be a hundred miles away while I'm fighting off half a dozen angry men, who will be coming at me with torches and pitchforks when they find out I'm a fraud."

"That's a bit of an exaggeration, Dr. Frankenstein. I really think you should consider it, these men were promised money or college credit, can you imagine how disappointed they are going to be? Hell, who knows, some of them might sue. I really hope you consider it; Pops would be proud."

"I'll think about it."

So with great trepidation... I agreed to lead the course.

WEEK ONE

I was nervous as hell and not very well prepared. A teacher of eleven and twelve-year-olds can get away with coming up with a lesson on the fly. I taught that way more often than I would like to admit. My problem with preparing for these adults was the fact that I didn't know where to begin, and honestly I was still grieving. I kept trying to approach it like I thought Dad might have. Although honorable, wouldn't work for me. My father and I were very close, but we had our differences. In the end, I decided I should approach the six men like I would a class of sixth graders. Giant sixth graders with facial hair who were all dealing with some sort of loss. How much different could they be? The objective should be nearly the same... help them grow.

I had to take care of some prep work in the classroom before the men arrived. I arranged the desks in a semicircle so they could face each other as well as the screen. On each desk, I placed a syllabus that listed all of my contact information and a list of all of our meeting dates. A projector was already in the room, I just needed to hook up my laptop to it to check to see if it functioned properly. Lastly, I needed to set up a video camera to record the sessions, (as part of their contract the men had agreed to this).

Each man came in one at a time. As they came in, I shook their hands and introduced myself to them by first name only. The first four were relatively early, the fifth arrived right on time and the last, a rather disheveled character, came in five minutes late. I busied myself by pretending to look over my notes. I cleared my throat and introduced myself again to the whole group.

"Hello, like I said, I'm George, George Samuel..."

The disheveled late arriver broke in, "Ya looks a helluva lot younger than the first time we met."

"That was my father, George Samuel *Senior*. I'm Junior. I'm sorry to inform you that he died two weeks ago."

A tall man with a faded ball cap was the first to speak, "I'm sorry for your loss. I just met him the one time, but you could tell he was a good soul."

I'm going to like this guy.

"Thank you, yes; he was a good soul and a great father. My family and I miss him terribly."

The men nodded their sympathies. A large scary looking dude dressed in black was the next to speak.

"Yes, sorry for your loss," he said in a deep, yet quiet, rumble, "I liked your dad right away. Perhaps this workshop will be therapeutic for you as well?"

"I never thought about that … you're probably right."

A heavyset fellow asked, "I don't mean to be rude, but how did your father die?"

"He died doing one of his favorite things. He-"

The disheveled guy broke in again, "Die in the sack did he?"

The remark threw me for a beat, as did the smirk on his face.

"No… he died in his study… reading a book."

A longhaired guy, a kid really, tried to lighten the awkward moment.

"I guess it was good that his favorite thing wasn't flying jumbo jets."

This threw me as well, until I realized his intention.

"Uh… yes… good thing."

"I'm sorry," the kid said, looking remorseful, "that wasn't very respectful."

"No harm done," I said, "Dad had a great sense of humor. He would have thought that was funny."

The annoying guy again, "We still gonna get paid?"

The guy was starting to piss me off, but I remained calm.

"Yes, nothing has changed except the facilitator. My approach will be different from my father's, but I, like he, expect a positive experience. Is everyone okay with me taking over?"

All the men nodded that they were okay with it.

"Great, let's get rolling. First of all, as you read in your contract, confidentiality is crucial. What's said in here stays in here…Now, let's start with introductions. As you all know, I'm George. I teach sixth grade here in the city. I'm married with two young sons. I went to school here and have lived in the city my whole life. How about we just go around the circle and tell us your name and a little bit about yourself?"

The tall man with the ball cap was to my right and the first to speak. He looked to be in his late fifties. He's lean and muscular, somewhat like an athlete but more like someone who works hard. I would guess he's well over six feet tall. He must work outside; he is tan and his olive colored t-shirt and blue jeans are faded from the sun. His cap is plain, nondescript, the color of sand, with smudges of grease on it. What hair you can see is cropped short and iron gray. He has a pleasant, quiet yet confident manner about him.

"Hi, I'm Ed," he said. "I'm a retired cop. I live on a small farm just outside of town. My writing experience was mostly limited to writing citations and filling out reports, but I'm looking forward to doing something more creative."

Ed was very brief with his introduction and I wanted to ask him if he had a family but I thought better of it. If he wanted to share more, he would have.

"Thanks, Ed. Nice to meet you."

I nodded to the next man. He was probably the most intimidating man I have ever seen, Johnny Cash on steroids. He was dressed in all black, black jeans, black steel-toed boots, and a long sleeve black tee shirt. The shirt was loose fitting, but it could not hide that he was powerfully built. His neck was thick and shoulders broad. His hands were the size of catchers mitts with jagged white scars covering the knuckles. He also wore his hair short but it was as dark as a raven's wing. His hair was a stark contrast to his intense pale blue eyes. He spoke slowly and quietly, not as if he was dimwitted, but like a man who thought before he spoke.

"I'm Daniel," he said. "I've only been in town for a couple of months. I have a habit of not staying in one place too long. I work at a bar down the street."

Like Ed, he didn't offer up a great deal of information about himself. I was totally okay with that. I was glad he spoke. I was glad he could speak. I was glad he didn't grab me by the neck when he saw me looking at his hands.

"Great; thanks, Daniel."

The next guy up was middle-aged, average build and size. His skin was dark and his curly hair was black, peppered with gray. It would be difficult to pinpoint his ethnicity, not that it mattered. He wore wrinkled khakis, a short sleeve dress shirt and a loosened tie. He looked a little worn out as if he was struggling with life just a little bit, and life was getting an upper hand.

"Hello, I'm Leon. I'm also a teacher. I teach American History at Central High School. I am a single dad trying to raise... three teenagers. I was born in the Dominican Republic, but I don't remember much about it. My family immigrated to the States when I was three years old. If you are wondering if I'm any good at baseball...I'm not."

Most of the men laughed at Leon's last comment. In spite of his haggard look, he seemed like a good person. He paused for just a bit when he talked about raising three kids and his voice started to catch. I would assume that his grieving has something to do with his children or the fact that he is single. In time, perhaps we will find out. Regardless, it was nice to have another teacher on board. Teachers are often self-conscious teaching in front of other teachers but right now, that was the least of my worries.

"Thanks, Leon. If we break into teams for a ball game, I won't pick you."

My stab at humor was not received as well as Leon's, but at least I made an attempt. The next man up was the one who had made the joke about Dad flying a plane. He was much younger than the rest of the men. He was dressed like one of my own kids; baggy gym shorts, sweatshirt, a well-worn Pirates ball cap, and black high top Chuck Taylor's. He was tan with long, wavy, light brown hair that fell across one of his eyes. He had the face of a baby with the exception of a few scruffy hairs on his chin. I would have been nervous at his age but he acted as if he fit right in. That was a good sign, if people were nervous or intimidated they would struggle producing quality work.

"Hi fellas, I'm Matty. I'm a junior here at the university. I was born and raised just outside of Pittsburgh, so I'm a big fan of the Steelers, the Pirates, and the Penguins. Please don't hold that against me. I'm working my way through school, picking' up odd jobs whenever I can. I'm a journalism major and hope to be a writer or maybe a sports reporter someday."

"Thanks, Matty. You are obviously the youngest member of the group. It will be nice to have the perspective of a young man in our discussions. Welcome."

I look at the next dude and can't wait to hear from him. He's the rude wiseass who gives the vibe that he is just interested in this workshop for the money. Although he has managed to immediately get under my skin, I want to trust that Dad knew what he was doing when he selected him.

He is scrawny, short, with pasty white skin and a large narrow nose. His flaming red hair is long, thin and wispy. It is brushed up and back. He looks like a candle blowing in the wind... no, that's too kind, he looks like a rooster riding in a convertible. He is wearing a dark blue work shirt and pants covered with oil and grease stains. The only clean spot on his shirt is over his right breast pocket where a name patch once was. Over the other pocket is a patch that reads 'iffy Lube'. I wonder if the 'J' was torn off for a comedic reasons or it's just a case of irony. He is slouched in his chair as if he's bored.

"I'm Ishmael," he smirks, "Folks calls me Ish."

My thoughts went to Ishmael from the Bible then the Ishmael from *Moby Dick*, and I blurt out.

"Call me Ishmael."

A confused look came across the face of Ish.

"I thought ya said your name was George?"

Leon, the teacher, quickly came to my rescue. Well, sort of. He actually made the situation worse.

"*Moby Dick*."

The confused look on Ish's face turned to one of anger.

"What did ya call me?" Ish said through gritted teeth.

Great start. I've got a guy pissed off during the first ten minutes of class. 'Hey Dad, if you're out there somewhere observing all of this, are you wincing... or laughing?' Luckily, Daniel, whom one would assume is a bouncer, intervened with a one-word whisper. His calm demeanor and apparent intellect were in stark contrast to his hulking physical presence.

"Melville."

Ish, confused, then angry, is confused again.

"Melvin who?"

"*Melville*, Herman Melville," Daniel, the big man in black, said, "'Call me Ishmael' is the first line of the first chapter in the novel *Moby Dick* by Herman Melville."

"It's a classic," Leon adds.

"It is considered a classic now but sadly he did not have much success during his lifetime," Matty, the young kid, said, "He was not considered a great writer until about thirty years after his death. I have a paperback copy of *Moby Dick* if you would like to borrow it."

Ish turned his head sideways and had a look about him as if he was in deep thought. I'm sure this was a look that did not happen often...

"I've hearda that story of course." he said, "I'm kinda busy right now, but

I might give that book a try."

Matty continued, "Most people think 'Call me Ishmael' is the first line of the entire novel, but it's really just the first line of the first chapter... like the big man said. The first line of the beginning of the book is; 'The pale usher – threadbare in coat, heart, and brain; I see him now.' "

So do I... with red hair.

"Many artists have been inspired by *Moby Dick*," Daniel said, "Coincidently; there is an exhibit of some of that art at the Cultural Arts Center down the street. I believe it's called *The Whiteness of the Whale*."

Matty offered, "That's the title of one of the chapters in the book."

"You know a lot about that book, kid," Leon said.

"I had to study it at length in high school and dissect it again here at the university, last semester."

Ish interjected, "I gotta cousin, Jasper, who goes cruising for fat white chicks. He calls it 'White Whalin'."

Ed's face lit up a little. With a slight, sly grin on his face he turned to Ish.

"Perhaps your cousin was inspired by Melville as well."

Ish returned the grin as if he was in on the joke, but I doubt that he was.

"I reckon he was. My cousin is a pretty good reader."

That might be possible... if *Moby Dick* was also published in comic book form. I need to stop thinking these snarky thoughts and get the group back on track.

"Sorry for interrupting you, Ish. Please tell us more about yourself."

"Well, there's notta lot ta tell... I enjoys beer drinkin' and movin' the rock... that's what hip people calls shootin' pool. I'm between jobs right now so if ya know anyone who's hirin', let me know... And one more thing... I'm a single fella."

Single? How could a woman pass up a prize like this guy? A dude who likes to 'move the rock'. Dad, seriously, what were you thinking?

Only one more participant to meet, and he appears to be an... interesting fellow. He is a large man, not like Daniel large, large in a soft way.... Okay he's obese. He is wearing an ocean blue Hawaiian shirt covered with an army of tiny hula dancers. The shirt is big enough to drape over the island of Maui, but does not hide his girth. On a face that is puffy and feminine, he is wearing rather thick glasses. His skin is pallid; it appears as if he has never been in the sun for any extended amount of time. A less professional person would find it ironic that we were just discussing a white whale.

"I'm Wayne. I am a computer programmer for an insurance company. I am recently divorced."

Ish let out a snort, "You was *married*?"

"Yes, for five years."

Ish turned his head to the side again but was still looking at Wayne.

"To a *woman*?"

The room became deathly quiet; the only sound was Wayne's labored breathing. This Ish was something else. Wayne was slow to answer, but his voice was even and under control. He took off his glasses and cleaned them on his shirttail.

"Yes... to a woman. I'm trying to date again, but it's not easy. My ex-*wife* hurt me pretty bad."

"Sorry man," Ish said, "Good luck with the dating... Hey, my twin sister is not seeing anyone at this time."

Wayne had a stunned, incredulous look on his face but managed to speak after a moment.

"I'm good... I mean I'm currently in a new relationship... but thanks... I think."

"Just let me know if ya change your mind. She's a helluva good cook. She makes a Frito dip outta Velveeta and Spam that's ta die for."

"I'll keep that in mind."

Again, the conversation got off track, but I think every time it happened, the men unintentionally revealed a little bit more about themselves.

"Okay, thanks everyone. It's great meeting all of you. We have a lot to cover tonight so I think we need to get started. I'm sure we will get to know each other quite well over the next several months.

My plan was that before we started writing poetry we should read some good poetry first. Let's start with some of the simple, yet famous poems by William Carlos Williams. For copy write reasons, I contacted *New Directions Publishing Company* for permission to copy these poems. The first one is *The Red Wheelbarrow*."

• • • • •

The Red Wheelbarrow

so much depends
upon

a red wheel
barrow

glazed with rain
water

beside the white
chickens

•   •   •   •   •

I gave each man a copy of the poem to read on his own. After a few minutes, Ish was the first to respond.

"It's kinda short, I like that, but I'm not sure I gets it. Why's a wheelbarra and some chickens so important to the fella?"

"They might be important to a farmer," Matty said. He looked at Ed, "You live on a farm. Wouldn't that be right?"

"Yeah, I suppose it would be," Ed replied, "but I don't think he was talking about someone's livelihood. I think he was talking about the scene itself, the positioning and the contrasting colors of the objects he was looking at... somewhat like a photographer might do."

We all thought about that for a moment. Daniel, the big man, was nodding in agreement then spoke up.

"Normally that scene would go unnoticed or unappreciated, but if you keep your eye open, or more importantly, your mind open, the ordinary can become extraordinary."

"Very cool!" Matty said with a hint of excitement, "I've read that poem a dozen times, thought it was cool... quirky and weird, but still cool. I never thought about it like you guys just did."

"I really appreciate that perspective as well," Leon said, "It's interesting to analyze a piece of writing. I have my History students do it all of the time, but we have to be careful not to overanalyze. The poet Billy Collins wrote a poem about people trying to beat a confession out of a poem instead of just enjoying it."

"I agree," Daniel said, "In the art world people often focus on what an artist is trying to *say* instead of just appreciating the art. I read recently that Picasso was once asked about one of his paintings, what it meant, he said something along the lines of, 'We don't know what the birds are singing but we listen to them anyway. With art it's important that sometimes... we just look.'"

The men were nodding and smiling, they got what he was saying. He continued.

"If an artist arouses curiosity, starts a conversation, brings about joy or even anger, then they have succeeded. Then again, many artists don't care what you think, they just have this need to create. You can do both, analyze and appreciate, but I guess the important thing is to ask yourself, 'how does this make me *feel*'?"

"Wow, that's some deep stuff. Good, but deep," Leon said. "And you work in a *bar*?"

Daniel did not answer; he just gave a somewhat sad smile and a slight shrug of his massive shoulders. Leon stated what many of us were thinking. Daniel does not have the look, or occupation for that matter, of someone you would consider a deep thinker. Ed, as well, for that matter. I should know better than to judge a book by its cover. Dad would never have done that.

I had the feeling Daniel was a little uncomfortable, so I jumped in.

"Well, this led to a better conversation than I was anticipating. Good job, guys. I think we have reached the point where we are ready to write our own poems. We are going to ease into this by all starting with a common theme or starter line. Eventually I would like you to come up with your own theme or topic. I would like your first poem to start with the line 'So much depends upon.'"

"Does we have ta write about chickens, a wheelbarra', and shit like that?" Ish asked.

"No, write about whatever you want. Please keep your subject matter and language relatively clean, as stated in your contract. I know you are all adults and I'm not a big fan of censorship, but for some reason that's what Dad wanted, so I want to honor that. I think it would be helpful in getting to know each other if you wrote about something from your life, your perspective. I'm sorry to treat you like sixth graders, but I thought it might be easier, at least for the first couple weeks, if I gave you a starter line. If you are stuck, you might want to try to take some pictures first. One of the pictures might inspire a poem. With that being said, if you write a poem that you have trouble coming up with a picture for, don't force it. It would be better to have a poem without a picture than to force a pairing that doesn't work. Often words stand better alone. I know that for some of you this is going to be new territory. It's not only the product but the process that we want to work on. Now let's head to the Art Department to get some photography pointers and to borrow a camera if you need one."

The students in the Art Department were a big help. The men listened closely as they were taught the basics of how to use a camera, how to frame a subject, lighting, etc. The men asked good questions (even Ish) and experimented with the cameras before they left. Matty took pictures of the other men and acted like a fashion photographer. They played along and laughed. Wayne really got into it and struck some rather... interesting poses, which made the men laugh harder even though I don't think he was trying to be funny. I'm sure Ish would have made some sort of comment about Wayne, but he was too busy hitting on, and repulsing, one of the college students. I thought I was going to have to step in and rescue the poor coed, but Daniel put a beefy hand on Ish's shoulder and whispered in his ear... the unwanted flirting stopped immediately.

• • • • •

I had a difficult time trying to figure out what had happened to these men that would push them to seek help for grieving. None of them struck me as even being remotely sad let alone dealing with loss or grief. I wished my dad had been there to help me figure these guys out, but, had he still been here... I wouldn't have been. One thing for sure, this was going to be an interesting ride.

WEEK TWO

I had some administrative stuff to take care of before class started, but to my surprise all the men were already seated when I arrived. They were making small talk, which I took as a good sign that they were getting to know each other. It might have been also to help them calm their nerves. I'm sure most of them were apprehensive about sharing for the first time.

I couldn't help but notice that Ish had one heck of a black eye. His left eye was a dark purple and almost swollen shut. No telling how that came about. I'm sure there is a host of people that would like to take a poke at him.

"Great to see everyone again. I hope you all had success with your first assignment. I'm really looking forward to seeing what you came up with. Ed, could you start us off?"

"Sure."

Rain on a Saturday Morning

So much depends upon the rain
that taps on the roof and window

It's not just the rhythmic drumming
brings you peace

but the knowing that a dry hayfield
is finally getting relief

tomatoes, sweet corn, and zucchini
will be that much closer to the dinner table

and the dust that once covered a pickup truck
is now a muddy puddle on the driveway.

•   •   •   •   •

I'm not sure what I was anticipating, but he delivered a nice simple poem.

"Good job, Ed. That was a great way to get the ball rolling. I really like the poem, and the picture works with it perfectly. Thoughts or comments from anyone?"

"I really appreciate the simplicity and imagery it creates," Leon said.

Daniel, smiling, leaned back in his chair and ran his thick hand through his hair. "I agree. Great piece, Ed. I enjoy a good rain myself."

Wayne added, "I enjoy zucchini bread."

"When they are ready to harvest I'll make some bread and bring it in," Ed said with a grin.

"I'll bet living on a farm is pretty cool," Matty said.

Ed nodded. "I don't think I could live anywhere else."

Matty asked, "I have heard that working in a garden is almost 'Zen like' for many people, is that true?"

"I've never thought about it before, but I would say that is true for me. I enjoy all aspects of it, the tilling, the planting, the watering, even chopping the weeds. It brings about a sense of peaceful satisfaction." Ed paused and looked down for a moment. He let out a short laugh, and then continued. "I've never told anybody this before... but occasionally... I like to work in the garden with my bare feet. I like to feel the warm soil on my skin... I feel like I'm part of the earth."

"My parents were really into gardening, and I never understood why," Leon said, "Now it makes more sense. All I know is they made me pull up the weeds, which as a kid... I hated."

Ed let out a laugh, clapped loudly and vigorously rubbed his hands together. This startled Ish, whose eyes had been shut for the past several minutes.

"That's one of my favorite things to do," Ed said, "I wore out my hoe last fall and had to get a new one."

Ish let out a whoop, "Now we're talkin'!"

"Sorry, Ish," Leon said. "I believe he was still referring to gardening."

"That was my fault," Ed said. "I thought that comment might have perked him up a bit, he was startin' to doze off on us."

Ish stretched, yawned, then smacked himself in the face several times

"Had me a late night last night," he mumbled. "This poetry stuff tuckered me out."

I was reluctant to ask Daniel to share, not sure what I would say if he refused. As if he read my mind, he looked over and gave me a slight nod as if to let me know it was okay to ask.

"Okay, Daniel are you ready to share?"

"Yep."

A Full Moon and a Paycheck

So much depends upon
the juxtaposition of a full moon and a paycheck.
The only thing worse than a Crazy
is a Crazy with money in his pocket.

So much depends upon
your body language
as a drunk inches towards your face
with a wild look and kerosene breath.
Maintain eye contact,
arms at your side, not crossed.
Muscles in the face relaxed,
same with the hands,
don't forget the hands.
Clenched fists are an invitation for trouble.

So much depends upon the smile,
but just a slight smile,
nothing pisses off a Crazy more than
the thought of being laughed at.

So much depends upon
the calmness, tempo,
and register of your voice
that is just above a whisper
causing the guy to lean in to hear,
but not the entourage.

So much depends upon
avoiding a situation
that causes a wife, girlfriend, or
God forbid, a mother
spending her night in the waiting room
of the E.R. And I, suffering through
another sleepless night
on a bed of guilt
covered with a blanket
of regret.

• • • • •

"Wow! Great work, Daniel!" I embarrassingly gushed. I regained my composure and said, "You've painted a world most people are not familiar with. In addition, the photo is wonderful as well. The full moon we had this week was fortunate timing for you."

"Yes, I had to take it on my break at work. Made a lot of people nervous walking around a bar with a camera."

"That poem rocks man," Matty said, "But, I gotta ask, why would someone get in your face? No offense, and I mean this respectfully, but you're built like a gorilla. A guy would have to be nuts to start something."

Matty read my mind. You would have to be insane or have a death wish to cross this guy. I would imagine major confrontations were rare. Ed had been nodding, he shed some light on how these situations could happen.

"You would be surprised," Ed said, "Some guys like a challenge to see what they're made of, especially after they've had a few... liquid courage. I would venture to guess that that has been going on since men lived in caves and wore leopard skin clothes."

Ed paused, rubbed his chin, then continued.

"I really like the poem, Daniel; you've made art out of something most people would consider dark and dangerous. I totally get it too. When I was a cop, I learned from veterans that your body language can often either diffuse or escalate a situation. At the police academy they teach recruits how to de-escalate potential problems, but it's quite a bit different when you get into a situation where you have to think fast."

"It's good advice for teachers as well," Leon said, "I was taught to thoughtfully stroke my chin when a kid starts to get agitated. It makes you look relaxed, and at the same time your hand is near your face to deflect a punch."

"Are young people that bad nowadays?" Wayne asked with a frown.

"No. Kids haven't changed a great deal... just in some ways."

"In what ways?" Wayne asked.

"Many of them act more entitled than kids of the past, the use of foul language is more prevalent, and many, not all, are not quite as respectful.

Parents have changed, that's for sure. Shockingly, they will be the ones who sometimes get in your face. And of course you have to control your emotions or you could lose your job. The last thing I need is to be labeled the hotheaded Latino. Some of these idiots could use a good punch in the gut. That's what I'd like to do, but instead I just smile and nod and take it while on the inside I'm cursing. It's not good for your health or your self-esteem. I'll get off my soapbox and share my poem now."

Just Mark Answer C

So much depends on
how well these kids do
on these standardized tests
my evaluation
my status
my career
we've gone over the Constitution
till I'm blue in the face
you know the answer kid
stop sitting there staring into space!
It's answer C
just mark answer C
C, DAMN IT, C!
C!, C!, C!

•   •   •   •   •

The guys all laughed at Leon's poem. I probably laughed the hardest. Unless you are in the field, you don't really understand how much pressure some teachers are under.

"It's very funny," Ed said, "It sounds like teaching is as stressful as law enforcement."

"It might very well be, but I was speaking like a teacher in a general way. Personally, I don't worry about test scores and its relationship to my evaluation too much. I know it sounds like I've been bitching about my job tonight, but I actually enjoy it, most days are pretty rewarding."

"As a fellow teacher I really see the humor and truth of your poem," I said, "Well done."

Leon smiled and seemed to sit a little taller. He probably enjoyed the praise and was relieved to have this over with for tonight.

"Thanks," he said, "I appreciate that."

Looking a bit uneasy, Wayne said, "I'll go next if that's okay."

"Sure, sounds good," I said.

The Mashed Potatoes

So much depends
upon

the creamy mashed
potatoes

glazed with dark
gravy

beside the fried
chicken

•   •   •   •   •

Wayne's poem was a great spoof of the William Carlos Williams poem I had shared with them last week. The men all chuckled and shook their heads. Oddly, Wayne sat relatively stone-faced, in spite of the positive reaction to his work. Nervous, perhaps.

"That's really clever, Wayne," Daniel said.

"Thank you."

"Yes, that's an interesting spin you put on that," Ed said. "Old William Carlos Williams would be proud. Don't you think, George?"

"Yes, I think he would be flattered. I assume he had a good sense of humor."

Ish was squinting at the poem and picture with his one good eye. His face broke into a grin. I braced myself for the comment he was about to make.

"Thata picture of your dinner, Wayne?" Ish smirked.

"Yes, it's what inspired the poem. I like to cook... and to eat."

"No shit?" Ish asked with a laugh and a slap on his thigh.

I didn't like where this was heading so I tried to quickly move things along.

"Okay Ish, why don't you go next?"

"Why not? I wrote it at the bar Daniel works at. I hope y'all likes it."

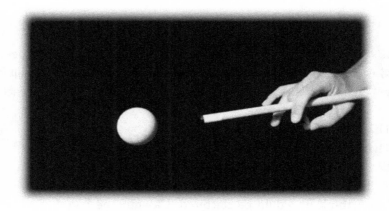

The Shot

So much depends upon
sinkin' this shot
in the right side pocket.
I got a twenty ridin' on this,
a twenty I failed to mention... I don't got
I desperately needs ta make this shot,
my beer's flat,
I'm outta smokes,
and this dude, impatiently
waiting for me ta shoot,
is a big sum bitch.
Can't rush this,
gots ta line it up just right.
Hard ta do seein' as how
a small crowd has gathered 'round,
and sasquatch is a tap, tap, tappin'
his size 15 boots
on the beer-soaked
wooden floor
to the same rhythm of the slappin'
of his pool stick in his meaty paw.

RICK THORPE

Well, here goes...
I draws back and
make a clean strike
on the cue ball just
as a bead o' sweat falls
from the tippa
my nose
to the green felt below.

•   •   •   •   •

We all sat in stunned silence, with the exception of Daniel who seemed amused. I was not expecting Ish to write anything, let alone something that was not half bad... somewhat crude, but interesting.

"Wow, Ish that's really good," Matty said.

"Thank ya. I'm proud of it."

"I like the photograph," Wayne said, seemingly trying to bury the hatchet. "It looks like you used a hand model."

"Had to ask the barkeep to pose for it. Daniel's hands is too scarred up, and most everyone else had dirty fingernails."

"Did you make the shot?" Leon asked.

"Nope."

"Does that explain the shiner?" Ed asked.

"Yep."

"Gambling can lead to ruin," Wayne said with a look of disapproval.

"Overeatin' can lead to diabetes," Ish said.

"I have a slow metabolism."

"And I'm a freakin' brain surgeon."

"Then you shouldn't have any trouble finding a job," Wayne murmured, looking off in the distance.

As humorous as this battle of words was, I was afraid it was going to get ugly fast. They were not shouting at each other yet, so I thought I'd better intervene before it came to that.

"Okay gentlemen," I said, "let's just stick to the poem. Ish, I agree with Matty. That is a good poem."

"Thank ya," Ish said, "Well, to be honest with y'all, I struggle a bit with readin' and writin'. I got a *lotta* help from my new friend Daniel here."

That explained why Daniel was not as surprised as the rest of us. He had something to do with the poem. That helped explain some things, but I was still curious to learn how Daniel had helped.

"No kidding?" I said. "How did that come about?"

"Well, I swung by his bar ta shoot some pool. Got ta feelin' confident man. I was draining' shots left and right. I'm tellin' y'all, I was hotter than a two-dollar pistol, so I make a bet with this big Chewbacca lookin' fella. Daniel kept

70

that dude from killing me, when I couldn't come up with the cash. Then Daniel paid the dude the twenty I owed, and escorted him out the door. Then he suggests to me I writes my poem about what just went down. So we get some bar napkins and a pen and he helps me knock out what he called a rough draft. I think he called it a rough draft, because it's hard as hell ta write on a bar napkin. We worked on that thing for a *long*, long, time. Almost half an hour! Then he met me at the library the next day ta type the thing up."

"Is that true, Daniel?" I asked.

"All in a day's work."

"Sounds like what we educators call, a 'teachable moment'," Leon said.

"I guess you could say that," Daniel said. "It was entertaining as hell, that's for sure. It was like a remake of that old Paul Newman movie, *The Hustler*. But instead of Fast Eddie and Minnesota Fats we had Slow Ish and Minnesota Large."

"Let me guess," Ed asked, "you let the guy get that one lick in on Ish because you thought Ish had it coming?"

Daniel had the slight grin again and laughter in his blue eyes. It appeared as if these two were going to get along well. Ed was not intimidated by Daniel's size and presence, and seemed to understand him better than the rest of us did.

"All part of the 'teachable moment'," Daniel said.

"It weren't one of my finer moments," Ish said.

"It *wasn't*," Wayne corrected.

"Not sure how you would know that," Ish snapped, "but thanks for agreeing with me, big boy!"

The men, with the exception of Wayne, chuckled at Ish's ignorance.

Ish thought the others were laughing with him and not at him. He beamed proudly.

"When I was a cop, I would sometimes let guys fight for a while before I broke it up," Ed said.

"Like in hockey?" Matty asked.

"Yeah, let them wear out a bit before I waded in... as long as no weapons were involved, of course."

"When I first started teaching," Leon said, "a wise veteran gave me some advice. He said, 'Never run to a fight, always walk. If you're lucky it will be over by the time you get there. We don't get paid enough to catch a punch or get your clothes torn.' Best advice I ever got. Unless it's a total mismatch or a bully is involved, I usually wait a bit before I break up a fight at school, especially if both kids are jerks. I have found if you establish a pecking order, they are less likely to fight in the future... at least with each other."

"Bystanders often read that hesitation as fear or apathy rather than patience," Daniel said.

"It can be a fine line," Ed said. "But I bet what others think doesn't affect your decision making?"

"It's not in my nature to concern myself with what others think," Daniel said.

Daniel looked down at his hands as he often does when he appears to be thinking. He did not elaborate anymore but I had to wonder if what he just said about himself was both a blessing and a curse.

"I think teachers, cops, and bouncers have more in common than people think," Matty said.

"At one point or 'nother in my life," Ish said, "I've had... *issues*... with all three."

"I doubt anyone is surprised by that revelation," Wayne said.

Ish turned his head sideways like he does when he is thinking, yet kept his eyes on Wayne. The shit-eating grin slowly spread across his face. It was payback time.

"Ever been inna fight, big boy?" Ish asked.

"Honestly, I've only had one scuffle," Wayne said, "and that was years ago... in high school."

"Kick some ass did ya?"

I was afraid of where this was heading, but at the same time I was curious as hell. So I, like the rest of the group, waited to hear what Wayne had to say.

"No, no... it ended rather quickly... uh,.. I was caught off-guard and I... and I... was slightly concussed."

"Gettin' cussed out ain't so bad," Ish said. "Happens to me every damn day."

"No... I was briefly... knocked *unconscious*."

"My bad. This is gettin' good! Keep talkin', big boy."

"Well..."

Obviously, Wayne was not comfortable with this and I felt like I had to step in and give him an out.

"You don't have to talk about it if you don't want to, Wayne."

"Ain't we tryin' ta getta know each other better?" Ish asked.

"It's okay." Wayne said, "It will feel good to get this off my chest. It would be humiliating if you all were my friends, but you're practically strangers. It all started as a little misunderstanding at band practice."

Most of the men showed little reaction so far. Matty covered his mouth with his hands, I would assume to hide a smile or muffle a laugh. Ish on the other hand was ready to have a field day.

"Hold up," Ish said, "Ya gots into a fight at freakin' *band* practice?"

"I told the girl next to me she was flat...and she misinterpreted what I meant."

I was afraid to make eye contact with the other men. If any of them thought this was the least bit funny, I would burst out laughing. Not very professional of the facilitator of a group on grieving. I bit my lip and stared at my feet. Ish, of course, was not going to let this go. He let out a hoot, threw his head back, and slapped both hands on both knees.

"Ya got knocked out by a damn *girl*?"

"She struck me over the head with her clarinet."

"Damn bro, she must have been a badass," Matty said.

"She was the cleanup hitter on the softball team."

"Well that makes it a little more understandable," Ish said, "but I don't really consider that much of a fight. I can't wait to tell the fellas down at the bar this one!"

"That's not going to happen." Daniel said quietly but firmly, "His story does not leave this room. Confidentiality is a group rule... and my rule."

Ish looked at Daniel and saw that he was serious. He then glanced at Ed, who was nodding his head in agreement. A weight was lifted off my shoulders.

"You got it chief," Ish said.

"Please believe me," Wayne said. "I can defend myself if I need to; I just usually choose not to. By nature, I'm a very patient and tolerant person."

"Gots thick skin does ya?"

Ish gave a quick glance over to Daniel to see if the subtle dig was going to get him scolded. Daniel gave no reaction.

"That would be one way to put it," Wayne said, "Look, can we move on from this topic?"

This was my cue to regain control of the group.

"Yes, we need to move on. Thanks for sharing your work, Ish. Well done. Matty, you are the last one to share tonight."

"Alright," Matty said, "be gentle guys, this is my first time."

The Number

So much depends upon
getting her cell number
if I could send her a text...
no, no, no...
She needs to hear the sincerity in my voice.
If I could talk to her
for just five minutes or so
she would be smitten by
my charm, my witty repartee.
I picture it going down something like this...
"Hello"
"Hi, is this..."
CLICK
Let me start over...
So much depends upon
finding out her name...

.   .   .   .   .

Again, the men chuckled after reading the poem. I was beginning to wonder if Dad had not selected these men, in part, because he thought they were clever, and would be entertaining.

"Another good piece using humor," I said. "I think we can all relate to that one."

Leon was grinning ear to ear.

"Oh to be young again. Is this something that's really going on right now?"

"Yeah."

"You get her name yet, kid?" Ed asked.

"Not yet," Matty replied.

"Man-up and introduce yourself," Leon said. "Sweep her off her feet... if people even use that phrase anymore. Whaddya got to lose?"

"My dignity."

"Kid, people introduce themselves every day," Ed said.

Matty paused and looked up at the ceiling before he responded.

"I know but I get all tongue-tied around beautiful women. Besides, I don't want to look like a creeper."

Ish pointed a grimy finger at Matty.

"Listen up, youngin'... I have found that ladies dig a fella with confidence... It works for me like a charm."

Wayne gave a little snort, and brought a chubby hand up to cover the smile on his face.

"Confidence and the fact that you're a sharp dressed man."

It wasn't clear if Ish picked up on Wayne's sarcasm. His eyes grew wide and he smiled.

"Hell yeah, just like the ZZ Top song!"

"Daniel, any advice for Matty?" Leon asked.

Daniel gave his sad smile and looked down at his hands. He rubbed the thumb of one large hand onto the palm of the other.

"Sorry, not one of my fields of expertise. But a wise man once said something to the effect, 'The most destructive force in the universe is regret'."

76

"Nietzsche?" Leon asked.

"Gibran?" Wayne said.

"Frank Zappa?" Ed asked with a laugh.

"Tommy Lee Jones, *Men in Black III*." Matty said with a confident grin.

"Bingo," Daniel said.

"So no regrets. Is that what you're sayin'?" Matty asked.

"That would be hypocritical of me to say that to ya kid," Daniel said. "I've had plenty of regrets in my life."

"This gal, she pretty hot is she?" Ish asked.

"Yeah, blonde, great eyes... killer legs, kinda long and thin... kinda bird-like."

"'Legs', another hit for ZZ Top," Daniel said.

"Had me a crush on a girl years ago, only had one leg.," Ish said with a far off look in his eyes. "Never would go out with me."

Leon had a mock look of astonishment on his face.

"No way, how could a woman resist your charm?"

"I hear ya. I always wonder what happened to ol' Eileen."

"Come on, Ish!" Leon said, "You knew a girl... with one leg... named *Eileen*? That joke is so old it came to America on the Mayflower. I think you're shittin' us. Pardon my language... let me rephrase that... I think you're pullin' my *leg*."

"I shit thee not!" Ish shouted. He jumped up and rolled up his sleeve. "I gots 'er name tattooed right here on my shoulder. Had my cousin do it in his garage."

"Ish, you don't spell Eileen, 'I- L -E –A- N'," Ed said.

"I know that... *now*, Farmer John! I showed her the tattoo thinkin' she might be impressed, but she up and dumped 'er beer right on my head. I tried splainin' to her my spelling skills... and my cousins, weren't so hot."

"Put her foot down did she?" Ed asked with a grin.

"She really didn't have much choice now, did she? She'd fall over otherwise."

"Your diction didn't impress her?" Wayne asked.

"Never got that far with 'er. She stormed out and I never seen 'er again."

"Did this romantic tragedy," Leon asked, "go down, with yet another ironic twist, at the IHOP?"

"Heck no! I hates pancakes. It happened in a bar."

"Not a surprise there," Daniel deadpanned.

"And she wouldn't go out with you?" Ed asked, "Ya musta not've showed enough confidence."

"I was justa young pup, still wet behind the ears, so ta speak…"

Leon had a mock look of seriousness on his face. He cleared his throat.

"If you could meet her again, now that you've matured, you would sweep her off her *foot*."

Daniel let out a short, deep laugh. He seemed amused at Leon's humor. He smiled again as he appeared to think of something that struck him as funny.

"I worked with a guy one time, a bartender, any time he sat down he would lean to one side. We thought maybe he was drinking on the job, or had a bad back. Come to find out he was born with only one ass cheek."

"Now that's different," Ed said. "Gluteus minimus."

"Yeah, and you would think that would be no big deal… but it was. He had trouble sitting, riding a bike, keeping his pants up…"

"Gettin' spanked," Ish interrupted with a smirk.

"I guess that means the poor fella missed out on havin' a butt crack," Matty quipped.

"I'm assuming it was more like a butt edge," Daniel said.

"On a positive note," Matty said, "I bet it was difficult to kick his ass."

I was surprised Leon had not jumped into the fray sooner, but I could see the wheels turning. Then, right on cue, he joined in.

"How was he as a worker, Daniel?"

"He did everything half-assed."

"Pretty good setup, am I right?" Leon asked.

"Yep, you're a great straight-man, Leon," Daniel said with a grin

"Thanks, my gay friends tell me that often."

The conversation was getting off course, but I felt as if it was helping build the chemistry of the group. I needed to redirect the conversation, and at the same time, I wanted to join in.

"Okay, Okay, I think we need to move on," I said, "No, ifs, ands, or *butts*…"

I was serenaded with a chorus of groans.

"Don't give up your day job," Leon said.

"Sorry I couldn't resist. Great job everyone. I hope you enjoyed this week's project as much as I have enjoyed reading them. I feel like we have gotten to know each other better after that. Here is another simple, yet popular, poem by William Carlos Williams, *This is just to Say*.

This is Just to Say

I have eaten
the plums
that were in
the icebox

and which
you were probably
saving
for breakfast

Forgive me
they were delicious
so sweet
and so cold

I handed out copies of the poem and we took several minutes to read it.

"It sounds like he is asking for forgiveness," Matty said, "but at the same time justifying his actions by saying how good they were, like 'How could you blame me?'"

"I bet his ol' lady was pissed about him eatin' them plums," Ish said.

"She probably got sick of him makin' a poem out of every note he left," Leon said. "*This is just to say, We are low on milk. I will pick some up. So frothy and white. Skim, perhaps two percent.*"

"She might have been flattered to receive poems from him all the time, to be included in his poetry world," Ed said.

"I'll bet you're right," Daniel said. "She might have been disappointed if he did otherwise."

"Did you notice how the title of the poem also acts as the first line?" I asked. "This poem has been imitated many times over the years by many different poets. Here are some examples. I think they are pretty clever."

These were handed out and read as well.

"Those are pretty cool," Matty said, "Is this going to be our next project?"

"Yes," I said, "I would like your title to act as your first line, and I would like your title to be; 'Please forgive me'. Feel free to make it serious, humorous, fictional, non-fictional, dark, whimsical, put any spin on it you want. And one more thing, this week I want you to submit your work anonymously, no names. Don't hold back for fear of embarrassment. Do whatever you want, just be creative. Any questions or comments before we break?"

"Oh, I almost forgot," Matty said while reaching into his backpack. "Ish, I brought my copy of *Moby Dick* for you to read."

Ish reluctantly took the well-worn paperback. He bobbed it up and down in his hand feeling the weight if it, then flipped through the pages. He handled and observed the book like it was a foreign object.

"Uh... thanks, kid. Damn... it's kinda thick."

"What a shame... no pictures!" Wayne added with mock surprise.

"I noticed that myself," Ish mumbled.

"Take your time," Matty said. "As a matter of fact I don't really need it back; I've read it several times. Sorry, it's kinda worn and the margins are filled with notes."

"No worries, kid. I've been known ta jot notes in books myself ...although my teachers didn't seem ta 'preciate that much."

"You can add it to your personal library," Wayne smirked, "...if there's room."

"Sure 'nough... *if* there's room."

"That reminds me," Daniel said, "I'm headin' to that art exhibit at the Cultural Arts Center, the one I told you about."

"Whiteness of the Whale?" I asked.

"Yep, I'm walking down there as soon as we're done. I usually like to go to exhibits and museums alone, but I'm in a rare social mood. Anyone interested in joining me?"

This was a great opportunity for the men to get to know each other better. I was really hoping the men would choose to go. I didn't want to be the only one to accompany the giant. Luckily, Ed came to my rescue.

"I'm in," Ed replied without any hesitation.

"I've got some time to kill before I pick up my youngest son at hockey practice," Leon said. "I'm in as well."

"I would love to join you guys, but I have a late dinner date I need to get to," Wayne said.

"I have a little studying I need to do, but I do want to see it," Matty said. "Maybe just for an hour."

All the men were staring at Ish, who seemed not to be paying attention to the conversation. He was tossing the copy of *Moby Dick* from hand to hand.

"Ish, you in?" Daniel asked.

"What the hell, I got nuttin' better ta do."

"Sounds like an impromptu field trip," I said. "Who knows, perhaps the exhibit will inspire some creativity. Let's go. Daniel, lead the way... please."

So that was the second night and their first night sharing their work. I could not have been more pleased with what they produced. It's an interesting, and, in an odd way, creative group. Dad knew what he was doing.

WEEK THREE

I arrived early with a box for the men to put their submissions in. I greeted each man as he came in and asked him to put this week's assignment in the box.

The impromptu field trip from the week before was pretty damn cool. The men seemed to enjoy the art and each other's company. Ish would often have a perplexed look on his face and just shake his head at some of the more abstract pieces. He would then wander off to flirt/harass with the girls who were working at the gallery.

There was a slight transformation in Daniel. He's hard to read and the change was pretty subtle, but he seemed... happier is the only way to describe it. He was engrossed in many of the exhibits and would look intently at things from many different angles. He went for long periods without saying a word, but he was willing to answer questions any of the other men had. The whole time he had a slight smile and his eyes were even more intense, if that was possible. It was odd but he seemed to let his guard down and didn't appear as intimidating.

"Sorry you weren't able to join us last week, Wayne." I said, "I think I can speak for... most of us... we had a *whale* of a good time."

Many groans and shaking of heads.

"I was able to go see it Saturday afternoon." Wayne said. "Very enlightening."

"Was it kinda like a family reunion?" Ish asked.

"Humorous but off base... as usual. The majority of my family is rail thin and olive complected."

"Adopted, was ya?"

"How about that giant origami?" Matty asked with excitement to no one in particular.

"Grandpap was stationed in Origami when he was in the service. I hear they're shuttin' his ol' base down," Ish said.

"I heard there was an article about Origami in the *paper* last week. Thanks for keeping us in the *fold*," Leon said straight-faced.

"Notta problem," Ish said, "I tries ta stay up on current events."

Before things got out of hand, I went ahead and turned on the projector with the first anonymous poem.

Please forgive me

For appearing in your dream last night,
but as I bounced from cloud to cloud,
I noticed your light was on
and your window was open.
The temptation was far too great.
So I sat on your sill like Peter Pan.
I should have lightly
rapped upon your window frame,
or rustled your curtains,
or quietly whispered your name.
But I couldn't bring myself
to wake you, you looked so...
peaceful

•   •   •   •   •

"Please don't try to guess the author," I said. "Just appreciate it, critique if you want, but I ask that you be kind."

"I love it," Leon said. "It's got a whimsical feel to it… if you can overlook the voyeurism aspect of it… if that's possible."

"It's kinda romantic," Matty said, "… in a weird way."

"It went south for me with the '*Peter Pan*' line," Ish said.

"I think you're trying to throw us off your trail with that comment, Ish." Daniel said with a sly grin. "I got a feelin' you wrote that poem."

Most of the group chuckled, including myself. Ish's eyes became two narrow slits, and he was clenching his teeth. He was clearly intimidated by Daniel, like the rest of us were, with the exception of Ed. Ish appeared to quickly catch himself and relax his posture as to not show too much aggression. You could tell he was still mad but he tried to control it.

"The hell I did," Ish mumbled.

Daniel was giving Ish a little taste of his own medicine.

"I bet under them jeans you're sportin' a pair of green tights," Daniel said.

"I ain't wearin' nothin' under these here jeans!"

"Too much information, dude," Leon said. "Please scoot over."

"Daniel, you know very damn well *I* didn't write that poem!" Ish said. "*You* helped me write mine!*"

"Relax brother, I'm just messin' with ya," Daniel said with a wave of his massive hand.

Ish was still steaming a little bit, and grumbling under his breath. He was sore at the big man but he didn't want to say anything to rile him too much.

"This is kind of embarrassing," Ed said, "but I loved the Disney Peter Pan animated movie when I was a kid."

"I loved his peanut butter," Wayne said softly with a laugh.

"I bet you had a crush on ol' Wendy, didn't ya Ed?" Leon asked

"She was too proper and uptight for me. Now I do recall thinking that Princess Tiger Lily was pretty cute."

All the men laughed with the exception of Ish who still wasn't quite over his irritation at Daniel.

"I had a crush on Betty Rubble," Wayne said.

"How can y'all have a crush on freakin' cartoon characters?" Ish scoffed.

"Well, Betty had a cute hairstyle and just an adorable laugh." Wayne said.

"Barney Rubble woulda whupped your ass!" Ish shouted.

"I do believe Barney played the clarinet," Leon said.

It took a few seconds for Ish to comprehend Leon's dig on Wayne. He then opened his eyes wide and his jaw dropped. He slapped both of his knees and pointed at Leon.

"Good one teacher boy!"

"Yeah, hilarious, teacher boy. I'm regretting ever telling that story. And by the way, Barney Rubble, for your information, occasionally played the piano and the drums, *not* the clarinet."

"I'm sorry, man... that wasn't cool. And... I stand corrected. I didn't know I was messin' with a Flintstone aficionado. How about you, Daniel? Any cartoon crushes?"

"We rarely had a TV that worked... but I do remember having a thing for that short girl with the funky sweater and glasses on *Scooby Doo*."

"*Velma*?" Leon asked, "Come on brother; how could you have a crush on Velma over Daphne?"

"Always had a thing for smart girls."

"Jinkies!" Matty said. "You should have pursued her Daniel... like you said... no regrets."

"Touché."

"Perhaps it's not too late," Leon said. "Have you seen her lately? She hasn't aged a bit."

"I think solving mysteries at night and staying out of the sun gives her that youthful glow," Ed said.

"Y'all are unbelievable," Ish said incredulously. "And I'm the oddball of this group? Right."

I was really enjoying this but once again, I knew it was time to redirect our focus. There was no point in hiding my smile so I didn't.

"C'mon guys," I said, "that was entertaining, but we really need to move on. I'm going to put another one up on the screen."

Please forgive me

for bustin' your jaw,
but you had gotten on my last nerve.
You need to learn when to
SHUT... THE... F*@%... UP!
My man, you really have a thick head...
in more ways than one.
If it makes you feel any better,
I busted up my hand pretty damn good.
Could be broke.

By the way,
I picked up one of your tooths,
at least I think is was yours,
from underneath your wheelchair.

I put the tooth in the pocket of my jeans.
If you wants it back,
I might have to check between
my couch cushions,
or the lost-n-found at the Laundromat.

•   •   •   •   •

"Wow, Ish!" Leon shouted, "You punched a guy in a wheelchair? That's low, brother."

"Who says *that* one is mine?" Ish asked, his voice rising. "Ya peckerwoods is startin' ta piss me off! And anyways, maybe the guy in the chair had it comin'! Ever consider that?"

"Your grammar and word choices give you away," Wayne said.

"It's nice to know you don't discriminate Ish," Daniel said.

"Thank ya, big man," Ish said with a hint of pride.

"I hope the guy had a good dental plan," Ed said

"Me too," Ish mumbled.

My plan to keep the authors unknown was flying out the window. I figured it would be easy to figure out Ish's poem. I just wasn't counting on the group members calling him out. A little disappointing.

"Just a reminder," I said. "These submissions were to be anonymous. Let's stick to critiquing the work. It defeats the purpose if we are calling guys out and judging their character."

"Yeah, remember that fellas," Ish sneered.

"Sorry, George," Leon said. "That was my bad."

"It's okay... let's look at the next one."

Please forgive us

We are having technical difficulties
with the system today
that we cannot quite pinpoint.

There will be periods of long delays,
slow service,
or no service at all.

We apologize for the inconvenience
this is causing
You will be notified via the intercom
when the system is up and running again
In the meantime, we suggest you;
shut down all devices,
look out the window at passing clouds,
or have tea with a co-worker,
daydream,
or write a poem

•   •   •   •   •

"Hey Ish," I said, "throwing your head back and making loud snoring sounds, is not really helpful criticism."

"Sorry," Ish said with a yawn, "but that one is a bit of a snooze."

"I like it," Leon said. "I think it's clever."

"Yeah, it's topical," Matty said.

"How so?" Ed asked.

Well, for example, if the internet is out, or there is no Wi-Fi or cell service, people freak-out. Many people don't know how to cope with being unconnected. I have a professor who complains about it all the time. He says we have become 'relationship poor' because of our addiction to screens. He claims, and he's right, that my generation is probably the worst, because we grew up with all that stuff."

"I don't have any of that shit," Ish said.

"You're probably better off," Ed said.

"My job would be extremely different without all that... *stuff*," Wayne said.

"Matty is right," Leon said. "At my school, teachers and kids freak out if the internet is out. Everyone scrambles for their cell phones, if they're not already on it. Give me a piece of chalk and a blackboard any day."

"Not a fan of cellphones?" Matty asked.

"It's a great tool and time saver. I need to have one to monitor my own kids. But at school, I found it was too big of a distraction. I was looking at it all the time. It was affecting my teaching. I leave it in the bottom drawer of my desk so I'm not tempted. I check for messages during lunch."

"Good for you, Leon," Ed said. "That sounds like a good way to deal with it."

I agree," I said. "That takes some discipline, Leon. Alright... here's the next one."

Please forgive me

For denting your fender.
I'm truly sorry,
but your car is so big
and this parking lot is so small.
You see, my rearview mirror has fallen off,
making backing up quite difficult.
Your car looks very expensive.
I assume you have a high-paying job,
with many perks and benefits.
Perhaps this is a company car?
I bet your trophy wife loves tooling around town in this baby.
Oh yes, please forgive these nosy onlookers,
who wrongly assume this note contains
my phone number and insurance information.
You see, I have neither.
I must close now,
for my six-pack is getting warm,
and I'm late for my first class.

•   •   •   •   •

"Matty, that is hilarious," Daniel said with a deep rumble of a laugh.

I started to protest Daniel guessing the author... but thought better of it.

"I agree, but I didn't write it," Matty said. "I think somebody is tryin' to set up the slacker young guy of the group. Well played... whoever you are."

"If I was the author of that one," Ed said, looking from face to face. "I would be grinning from ear to ear. Someone here has a great poker face."

"The guy in that poem behaves in a manner that we would *like* to, but never would," Leon said. "Well... most of us anyway."

"Why y'all lookin' at me?" Ish asked.

Wayne was shaking his head with a look of slight disgust.

"It sounds like a very irresponsible person to me."

"I repeat...Why y'all lookin' at me?" Ish asked again. "I think ya need to lighten up big boy... no pun intended."

"I believe someone was just using humor, Wayne," I said. "I believe I mentioned that humor was an option. From the conversations we have been having, I would say most of you are okay with that. All right, if there are no more comments, I'll put up the next one."

Please forgive me

for getting you the wrong flowers.
How unfortunate to have a rose allergy.
I guess that trip to Pasadena
is now out of the question.
Also, forgive me for the melted
box of chocolates.
I had no idea a dashboard could get so hot.
And of course I meant nothing by 'Sugar-Free'
it was the last box on the shelf.
I hope you had a nice Valentine's Day.
I know I sure did.
I can't thank you enough
for the pair of left-handed scissors.
They will come in handy someday,
if I ever decide to cut things
with my left hand.

•   •   •   •   •

With the exception of the sound of suppressed snickering from Matty and the delayed burst of laughter from Ish, the room was silent. I believe the awkward silence, from most of us, was because we were not sure if the poem was serious or not. I think because of that not knowing, people were reluctant to make comments. Being in charge, I broke the silence.

"Well, whoever wrote that one, thanks; it was... it was... well written, and the picture is outstanding."

"That was a humdinger!" Ish shouted.

"I think we can all relate to that one," Leon said.

"How so?" Wayne asked.

"Well, we've all probably had the experience of not getting the response we expect when we give someone a gift," Leon said

"It can be awkward," Ed said.

Wayne sniffed, slid his hand under his glasses and pinched the bridge of his nose. "Or downright hurtful," he said, his voice cracking.

"Yes, I think we all can agree with that," I said. "Okay... here is the last submission."

Please forgive me

for not saying goodbye.
I struggled to find the right words.

Forgive me for never telling you
how much I loved your laugh,
the shape of your mouth,
the expressiveness
of your eyes,
and the way
you carry yourself.

Forgive me
for never holding your hand,
brushing back your hair,
and kissing your cheek.
Forgive me for never properly....
Introducing
myself.

•   •   •   •   •

"Wow... the ending really threw me. It was, I don't know... real," Leon said.

"Real and somewhat sad," Ed said.

"Or just real sad. I feel sorry for that sucker," Ish said.

"Full of melancholy and..." Leon said, then paused to find the right word.

"Regret," Daniel whispered, looking at the floor.

"Yeah, regret," Leon said, "That seems to be a common theme with us."

"Ain't *that* the truth," Ish said.

"Well my hat's off to all of you," I said. "I loved that last poem... I've loved them all. There is a lot of talent in this room. Okay, here are several poems I want us to look at tonight. See if you can detect a theme."

We read several poems by various poets. Some older classic poems from Walt Whitman and Robert Frost and some more modern poems from Joyce Sutphen.

"Those are all great," Daniel said, "The first thing I noticed was that all of the poems are not necessarily about nature, but take place in nature, or outside at least. I think they all are inviting; the poet wants you to experience what he or she is experiencing."

I was looking for that response. Actually, it was better than the response I was looking for.

"Very good," I said. "For your next project I would like you to go outdoors for your inspiration. Perhaps go to a favorite place that might evoke a strong feeling or memory. Be patient if nothing comes to you. As I've suggested before, if you are having trouble, try taking a few pictures first. Sometimes the image you see will inspire a theme and then words will follow."

"Many poets have been inspired by pictures, paintings, and sculptures," Daniel said.

"True," I said, "and many artists have been inspired by poems."

So take that big boy, *I* know stuff too! I thought to myself, and would never dare say out loud to anyone (let alone someone as large as Daniel).

"The painter Charles Demuth made a cool painting based on a poem by his friend, and ours, William Carlos Williams," Daniel said.

Damn... twice as big as me... and twice as smart.

"David Hockney was a painter *and* a poet," Matty added.

"Yeah, his writing is pretty good," Daniel said.

"But he made *a bigger splash* in the art world," Matty said.

"Yes he did," Daniel said with a hearty laugh. "That was pretty slick, kid."

"Thanks, I was pretty proud of that. I was not sure if you were going to catch it or not. I'm not a Hockney expert; I just happened to read an article about him in *The Guardian*."

Not sure what Matty said to get praise from Daniel, and apparently neither did the rest of the group. They nodded and smiled at each other like they were the only ones getting an inside joke. I made a mental note to Google David Hockney and 'a bigger splash' later tonight.

"This assignment will be a breeze for Ed," Leon said. "I bet he's outdoors more than he is indoors."

"That's about right," Ed said. "I love that line from the Whitman poem you shared with us; *I think heroic deeds were all conceived in the open air, and all free poems also.*"

"Whitman was a rock star," Matty said. "Way ahead of his time."

"I'm not sure he was as appreciated as he should have been during his lifetime, like many visionaries," Daniel said.

"I just adore his chocolate samplers," Wayne said.

"That dude with the Santa beard (I had shown them a picture of Whitman) wrote poems *and* made chocolate?" Ish asked.

For once, I was somewhat grateful for Ish and his ability to lower the I.Q. of the conversation.

"I think Wayne was kidding, Ish," I said.

"Have you ever seen the movie *The Dead Poets Society*?" Matty asked. "I had an English teacher in high school who showed it to the class. It's life changing; I'm not exaggerating; it turned me onto Whitman. There is a poem read by Mr. Keating, played by Robin Williams, *Oh me, Oh Life*. The poem starts out with the narrator observing the depressing masses of people, and beating himself up for his own pathetic, meaningless life. It winds down like this: 'The question, O me! So sad, recurring- What good amid these, O me, O life? Answer'..."

Matty paused and looked around the room for dramatic effect. Before he could finish. Leon, looking out the window, finished the poem.

"'Answer. That you are here - that life exists and identity. That the powerful play goes on, and you may contribute a verse'..."

"Right on," Matty said with a grin.

"I have that poem taped to my desk," Leon said in almost a whisper. "It's pulled me out of dark times, more than once."

We were all quiet for what seemed like a long stretch of time, absorbing the quote and what Leon had just said. No one seemed sure how to respond. Wayne cleared his throat and broke the silence, and the reflective mood, with a change of topic.

"I'm not sure about this assignment," Wayne said. "My allergies this time of year are simply horrendous."

"Take a hanky, Spanky." Ish barked.

"I never leave home without one."

These two are hard to believe.

"Sorry about your allergies, Wayne," I said. "Do the best you can. Before we break for tonight, I want to play a song for you. It is an example of a piece of writing that was inspired by an outdoor experience. The song is *Nightswimming* by R.E.M. "

"That's a really good song," Daniel said, "I haven't heard it in years. I almost forgot about it."

"Yeah, great tune," Leon said. "Always reminds me of my youth."

"Never heard of it," Ish mumbled.

"Listen to it with an open mind and I think you'll see what I mean," I said. "I've printed off the lyrics for you and I found a version of it on YouTube that I really like. The lead singer of *R.E.M.*, Michael Stipe, sings it with Chris Martin and *Coldplay*.

"Never heard of them neither," Ish said.

"What century are you living in?" Matty asked.

"My car radio's been busted a while."

"For *twenty* years?"

"Sounds 'bout right."

"Let's listen to it, and we'll talk about it," I said,

I played the video for them twice so they could get a chance to absorb the lyrics. I think for the most part they enjoyed it.

"A blend of beauty and sadness," Ed said. "I guess thinking back on your past is often that way."

"I think it captures what many young people go through," Leon said. "Doing something risky or illegal can be scary and exciting... sometimes even romantic. The *imagery* it evokes is vivid, at least in my mind."

"The protagonist in the song is self-conscious like most young people are," Daniel said. "That line, 'They can't see me naked,' can be interpreted as, 'They can't see me, because it's dark' or 'I don't *want* them to see me because it would be humiliating.'"

"Our bodies are beautiful," Wayne said. "We should be proud of them."

"Keep your shirt on big boy... no pun intended," Ish said. "Are ya sayin' we all ought ta be paradin' around in our birthday suits?"

"As fun as that might be, it would be impractical and distracting. My point is... in appropriate settings... one should not be ashamed of being naked."

"Well, I know *one* fella that should," Ish smirked.

"Whitman celebrated the naked body in his poems," Daniel said. "Probably why he wasn't welcome with open arms back in his day... pun intended."

"This conversation is comically appropriate," Matty smirked.

"How so?" Leon asked.

"I'll give ya a hint; I just got the highest paying job that a student can get on campus."

"What's that?" Ed asked. "Lifeguard?"

"Close, that's the second highest paying job."

"Ninja?" Ish asked.

"Uh, no... I'm going to be a nude model for the art department."

"Wow, that desperate for money, Matty?" Ed asked.

I detected just a hint of fatherly concern in Ed's voice. I had the same feeling.

"Are there other jobs you would consider?" I asked.

"Yeah, sure... but honestly, the pay is really good, and I'm on a bare bones budget."

"Interesting choice of words," Daniel said.

"What would Freud say about that?" Leon asked with a laugh.

"Is Freud the drawin' teacher?" Ish asked with a puzzled look on his face.

"No, he left the stick figure department and now teaches ceramics," Daniel deadpanned.

"I believe it's watercolors," Ed said.

I was curious how long that they would keep this up before one of them laughed, or when Ish would catch on. These guys might do well at amateur comedy night.

"You guys didn't hear?" Leon asked. "He was transferred to the dance department."

"I stand corrected," Daniel said. "I'll even add a plié."

"I'd pay good money to see that," Ed said with a laugh.

Ish had his head turned sideways again, as if he was thinking.

"I think y'all are dickin' with me again."

Just over a minute to catch on. Not too bad.

"Sorry Ish," Daniel said. "Sigmund Freud was a famous Austrian doctor who was the founder of psychoanalysis."

"Oh.... we were talkin' 'bout *that* Freud... Ya shoulda said so in the first place. I thought ya was talkin' 'bout *Lucian* Freud."

"Who's Lucian Freud?" Leon asked. "I know he's famous for something."

"I'm aware of the work of Bella Freud, the designer, but I'm not as familiar with Lucian," Wayne said.

I didn't have a clue. Daniel looked around waiting for someone else to answer. He finally spoke up.

"That's comical, Ish. You know *Lucian* Freud but not Sigmund."

"Who was he?" Leon asked again.

"Lucian Freud was the grandson of Sigmund... father of Bella... He was a British painter whose work goes for millions... it did even when he was alive. Ironically, he was famous for his nudes. I'm guessing that might be why Ish was familiar with him. Impressive nonetheless."

"I ain't as shallow as y'all think," Ish said with a coy smile.

"Daniel, I still find it hard to believe... you work in a bar?" Leon asked. "You know more stuff than people I teach with, and I teach with some really smart people."

"I read a lot," Daniel said with a shrug, "You should be more impressed with Ish."

Ish was bobbing his head up and down with a cocky smile on his face. Just when think you have someone pegged... you don't have them pegged.

"Matty, would you know if there are any positions available?" Wayne asked.

"By *positions* I sure hope you mean jobs," Matty said with a look of shock. "Uh... I'm not sure... I'll ask about openings... I mean if any are available."

"Thinking of *moon*lighting, Wayne?" Leon asked.

"The girl I've been seeing is busy most nights," Wayne explained, "and I have been getting bored. Besides, she would like to go on a cruise, so any extra money I can bring in will go towards paying for that."

Wait for it...

"Maybe you and college boy could work together. Don't they sometimes pose in pairs, ya know, like with partners," Ish suggested with a wink and his trademark smirk.

Bingo.

"I believe this is a gig for one person," Matty quickly blurted out, "but *thanks* for your help Ish, I really appreciate it."

Round two.

"I don't mean to be o'fensive, Wayne," Ish said, trying to keep a straight face, "but ain't ya a little large ta be modelin'?"

"Once again you are a little out of touch with what's in vogue," Wayne said with a snarky tone. "Bigger models are now fully accepted, appreciated, and often sought after."

"If that's true then I'm *glad* I'm outta touch."

"Now, Ish... if you really were aware of Lucian Freud," Daniel said, arms folded across his massive chest, "you would know that many of his nudes were of very large people, both men and women."

"Musta slipped my mind."

"Let me get this straight kid... you are too shy to introduce yourself to a cute girl, but you'll pose in the nude in front of a room full of art students?" Leon asked.

"I know it's weird, I'm really not that shy, but she just makes me nervous. I was kinda hopin' the art department would let me wear a mask."

"You'd be like a naked superhero," Ed said.

"You'd better hope it's a drawing class and not a photography class," Leon said, "or you might end up being an internet sensation."

"What if that girl you're hot for is in that their drawin' class?" Ish asked leaning forward, wide-eyed.

"That, my friends... would be a total disaster."

"Be a shame for her to see your shortcomings before formal introductions were made," Daniel said.

"Wow... the big man is on a roll tonight!" Matty said.

Okay, time to take the heat off the kid.

"Speaking of jobs - any luck finding work, Ish?" I asked.

"Yes, as a matter of fact, I start deliverin' pizzas for a pizza joint tomorrow night."

"Which one?" Leon asked.

"*Beccaccio's*."

"I almost ate there once," Matty said. "I walked in... and walked right back out. Didn't the Health Department shut that place down?

"That was all a huge misunderstanding," Ish said, throwing his hands up in the air. "That rat died of natural causes. Tony opened 'er back up, last week."

"My students call that place *Salmonella's*," Leon said.

"That's a different Italian joint altogether," Ish said. "I believe it's over on Fifth Avenue. I've known the Monella family for years, Sal went to school with my oldest brother."

"My mistake."

"I can get y'all a three percent discount," Ish said, puffing up his chest.

"Wow, a whole three percent?" Daniel said. "I'd hate to take advantage of our friendship."

"Not a problem, Daniel. It's the least I could do after all ya done for me."

"Okay gentleman that will do it for this week," I said. "Good luck with this next assignment. Get a hold of me... or Daniel... if you need help with editing."

I didn't add much to the conversation tonight. I found it more fun to sit back and take it all in. I'm amazed at how comfortable these guys are with each after only three weeks. They praise each other and tease one another like a family. Dad would have made a great chemist. Daniel continues to baffle me with his vast knowledge and humor, in spite of looking like an escaped convict. The other men are doing well also. Sarcasm, subtle and unsubtle, abounds. Still not sure about Wayne - he's a hard one to figure out. I've come around to appreciating Ish a little; he is comic fodder for the other guys, and he takes it in stride. I really do not like the fact that he rides Wayne about his weight. However, Wayne gets his subtle jabs in as well. I need to say something to Ish. I would never let that go on in my sixth-grade classroom.

I'm not sure if any healing is going on, but they all seem to be enjoying themselves. (Myself included.)

WEEK FOUR

"Alright guys," I said, "I think we can start now that everyone is here. It's great to see you all. I hope everyone was able to get outside and get inspired with all this great weather we have been having."

"Speaking of inspiration," Leon said with a giant grin, "I wrote my poem early in the week so while I was still feeling creative, I wrote two more poems in honor of our two friends here, on their recent employment. Would that be okay, George?"

I had a feeling I'm going to regret this, but my curiosity got the best of me.

"It's okay with me if it's okay with Matty and Ish."

Matty had his head bent down and was shaking his head, but you could see a slight grin. Ish looked startled when I said his name.

"Go for it," Matty said.

"Well sure, teacher boy," Ish said. "Ain't never had anybody write a poem for me. I might get a little choked up."

"Cool, thanks fellas," Leon said. "This first one is also with a nod to Dr. William Carlos Williams."

"William Carlos Williams was a *doctor*?" Ish asked.

"Yes, a baby doctor," Leon said.

"Like Doogie Howser?" Ish asked.

"No Ish, he... Uh yes, like Doogie Howser. Here's the first poem."

The Red Mini Van

So much depends upon
a red minivan
beside the white SUV
stopped at the intersection

The driver, of said minivan,
can see me coming
has ample amount of time
 to pull out in front of me
but does not....

They wait
perhaps they sense my urgency
to get to my next customer and lousy tip
or maybe they can just feel my need, my passion
for unconstrained speed

RICK THORPE

They rightly assume that under the hood
of this crumpled '81 Ford Escort beats
the heart of a tiger,
a 1.6 liter, 65 horses of unbridled fury

Maybe that driver has assumed,
due to the pizza delivery sign on my roof
that my braking system is shot to hell,
dangerously low on brake fluid or pads worn paper thin...
both are correct assumptions

I'm close enough now that they can see my
thinning red mane blowing in the breeze
due to a window that won't roll all the way up

In me, they see a version of James Dean,
an older, scruffy version
but a version nonetheless
not in an old-ass '81 Ford Escort
but in a '55 Porsche 550 Spyder

So here's a toast...
to you Red Mini Van
I raise my oversized plastic cup
in your general direction
I thank you and salute you...

But wait....
What are you doing?
You can't be pulling out now!
I'm almost to the intersection doing
a reasonably safe five miles over the posted speed limit!

Why? Why did you wait so long?
Okay, so the reasonable thing to do

when pulling out in front of someone
is to quickly accelerate,
but no, you pull out
with the speed of cold maple syrup!
My barrage of curse words falling on deaf ears
as my cigarette falls on my crotch
thus more swearing coupled with left of center driving.

And you don't even have the decency to look
in your rearview mirror to see the scowl and knitted brow.
Until now, my love for you was unadulterated
We had it all red minivan, we had it all...
but you threw it away red minivan
like the Big Gulp cup
I've just tossed out the window...

•   •   •   •   •

"Very creative, Leon," I said. "I'll admit I was a bit worried at first, but that was very, very good."

"Clever," Wayne said dryly, "but perhaps a little too articulate if speaking in the voice of a pizza delivery man."

"And the picture is artistic as hell!" Matty said excitedly. "Did you lie down on the road to take that? That could be dangerous."

"Yeah, speakin' of which. You think anyone stopped when they saw a black man lyin' on the road? Not one person. One guy drove real close; tried to finish me off."

"For real?" Matty asked eyes wide.

"Nah, I'm messin' with ya kid. No cars went by. I didn't even take the picture. I had my school clothes on, had my son take it while I watched for traffic."

We all broke into laughter.

"Bravo, Leon," Daniel said, "I assume you were emotionally drained after that one."

"That was darn good," Ed said. "What do you think Ish, was he accurate?"

"Well I'm flattered, but let me clear up some inaccuracies. First of all... I don't drink no Big Gulps... I prefers a Slurpee..."

"Me too," Wayne said.

"I believe that is the first thing Wayne and Ish have ever agreed upon," Ed said with a look of mock shock.

"I have heard that a Slurpee is good for a hangover but Slush Puppies are better," Matty said. "Is that true, Daniel?"

"I've heard that also, but I don't know if it's factual."

"When I was a kid 7-Eleven called their slush drink an Icee," Ed said. "What's up with that?"

Ish looked as if he was getting frustrated that the topic had veered off.

"Hold on fellas! I weren't done talkin'... *Secondly*... I don't drive no freakin' Escort, that's for wimps. I drives a nineteen seventy-three Ford LTD."

"Let me guess... rusty as all hell?" Daniel asked.

"Yeah, she gots a little rust. The feller who gave it... I mean the guy who I bought it from... suggested I get me a tetanus shot."

"Please forgive my inaccuracies," Leon said. "I might have been using a bit of a poetic license."

"Speaking of license…" Daniel said with a pause, "Ish, when you first came to my bar and I was messing with you and ask to see some ID, you hemmed and hawed, and patted yourself down like you had forgotten it. Do you even *have* a driver's license?"

"Well…It's a long story, and I don't want to bore y'all with it. Let's just say I'm lookin' into that."

"You're lucky I'm not still a cop, buddy," Ed said.

"Hypothetically, if you still were a cop, and you pulled Ish over," Daniel said, "would you have performed a body search for weapons? You know, just to be safe."

"Probably not," Ed said. "I didn't like to mix business with pleasure."

"You must have been a model of constraint," Daniel said.

"A true professional," Leon added.

"Now look y'all…," Ish started to say.

"Do you still have your handcuffs?" Wayne interrupted.

"Uh… no… I believe I turned my bracelets in when I left the force."

"That's a shame," Wayne said, disappointment written all over his face.

I thought it best to redirect this conversation before Ish had time to comment.

"Okay, moving on… Leon, you said you had two bonus poems for us tonight?

"Yes," he said, "This next one is for the kid… Sorry pal."

"I can hardly wait," Matty groaned.

The Silent, Unencumbered Thoughts
of a Nude Model on His First Day

'This is humiliating; I haven't had this many snickers since Halloween...'

'My parents were right, what good is a degree in Philosophy?'

'There has got to be a better way to make twelve dollars an hour...'

'I wonder if they will pay me by cash or check... and where will I put it?'

'At least I'll save on dry cleaning...'

'In all the history of nude people I'm sure no one was ever in this pose...'

'Whatever *that* is... I need a doctor to look at it..."

'Should have done more crunches...'

'Does this mean my luffa sponge is now a tax write-off?'

'I think I'll leave this gig off of my resume...'

'You've been staring long enough Mrs. Robinson, start sketching...You too buddy!'

'I wonder ... does the lack of pants make my butt look fat?'

'The custodian chooses now to empty the trashcan? Could he at least have closed the door?'

'If the temperature in this room drops one more degree, you all are going to need erasers...'

'Other jobs I wouldn't want to do in the nude... Fry Cook, Cat Groomer, Welder, Hockey Goalie...'

'What in the hell is Kwame smirking at?'

'It does not itch, it does not itch, it does not itch, it does not...'

'Add to shopping list... disposable razors, coconut oil, hemorrhoid ointment.

'I just had to have a third refill on that iced tea...'

'Do *not* think about the blonde in the third row, Do *not* think about the blonde in the third row, Do *not* think about the blonde in.........,

Damn it!'

•   •   •   •   •

"Outstanding!" Ed said while clapping... "*Absolutely* no pun intended. You are running on all cylinders tonight, Leon."

"I have no doubt that you are a good teacher, Leon," Daniel said, "but I think you missed your true calling."

"Thanks, fellas," he said.

"Most of your poems have an air of frustration. Do you have anger issues?" Wayne asked.

"Yep."

The men laughed at Leon's brief and honest reply.

"As funny as that poem is... at my expense... it's not too far off of the truth," Matty said. "I wasn't going to share this, but yesterday was my first day on the job. I was given some advice before I started, 'Look at a spot on the wall or the floor and focus on it, that will help you avoid eye contact with the people who are sketching you.' That's easier said than done."

"Let me guess, Daniel said. "You looked at the artists and wondered what they were thinking?"

"Exactly. It was easy to tell the first timers, they were as uncomfortable as I was, maybe more so. I need money for tuition and to pay bills, but the job has more drawbacks than the obvious one, humiliation."

"Such as...?" Leon asked.

"Well, nude models can't study or work on assignments while on the job like many campus jobs."

"If they could, it would potentially have made artwork titles more interesting," Daniel said, "Instead of *Nude Descending a Staircase*, Duchamp's masterpiece might have been, *Nude Cramming for Econ Exam*."

Leon jumped in, "*Nude Highlighting a Textbook*."

Then Ed, "*Nude Painting a Nude*."

"That was good, Ed... deep," Leon said.

"Thank you, I think you guys are rubbing off on me."

I would have loved to join in on this conversation, but I was having too much fun just observing and listening. And honestly, I don't think I could think fast enough to join in.

"Honestly guys - I'm not sure I'll last at this job very long," Matty said.

There's your openin' *De*Wayne," Ish said with a cackle.

"I know you think it's comical, Ish, but I just might apply."

"Hope they gots *real big* drawin' paper over there at the art school!"

"A lesser man would say, 'Bite me'," Wayne murmured through gritted teeth.

"Sorry, no can do, the doc from the clinic, has me on a low-fat diet."

Wayne took a deep breath and blew it out slowly. Ed glared at Ish, and Daniel wagged his finger at him and shook his head. Ish threw up his hands in surrender. Just when a person becomes less of an ass, he becomes... *more* of an ass.

"Let's stay on topic, guys. I don't mind when we get sidetracked or when we rib each other, but I insist we stay positive and not say hurtful things. Am I clear, Ishmael?"

"Whatever, boss."

"Leon, can you present your assigned poem please?"

"Sure, George."

Better than a Picnic

Stretched out under the grass under my favorite oak
a book about the Civil War lies open out before me.
I'm starting to doze off ... I notice a small brown ant crawling across page 209.
He is heading toward the picture of William Tecumseh Sherman.
Sherman's steely gaze widens as the ant approaches.
In serpentine fashion he makes his way across the page
And parks himself right under Sherman's nose.
The general's eyes widen in disbelief.
Growing visibly agitated, Sherman tries to rid himself of the pest.
Brushing away the beast is not an option.
He's a portrait made up of just head and shoulders, lacking hands.
Twisting his lips and scrunching up his face is futile, and not very dignified.
One can sense he is ready to perform an act bordering on desperation;
To embark upon a tactic well beneath a man of his fame and stature.
Sherman takes an enormous inhale and fills his chest to capacity.
(No easy task for a two-dimensional person wearing a rather snug coat)
Cocking a nostril towards his target he blows a mighty blast of air (and dust).
His aim is true; the ant scurries on more out of annoyance than injury or fear.
A less than confident smirk appears on Sherman's face.
A worthier foe he has not faced in more than seven score.
Next door on page 210, General Grant lets out an obnoxious snort.
He's so amused and distracted that he spills the shot of whiskey he is holding.
A few drops of amber liquid drip from the portrait and down the page.
It splashes onto a picture of a smoldering Atlanta and evaporates with a hiss.

The ant heads towards Grant and now Sherman is the one who is bemused. Without batting a half open eye, Grant lifts his cigar to his lips and draw deep. The stogie glows a vibrant red; a stark contrast in a black and white picture. He removes the cigar from his mouth and points it at the slim-waisted foe. The ant stops dead in his tracks, even his elbowed antenna freeze in place. Sherman nods, impressed by the cool-headed, quick thinking leader; musing-'Lee didn't stand a chance against that guy'.

• • • • •

"That was so bizarre, so surreal... I love of it!" Matty said. "How did you come up with that?"

"Thanks. Well, this is gonna sound a little weird, but I was under a tree with a textbook during my lunch period, just like the poem starts out. Sure enough, an ant walks onto the page. I got the idea, and started writing the rough draft like a lunatic. I was late getting to my sixth-period class."

"Did ya eat some funny mushrooms while ya was lyin' there?" Ish asked.

"I think it's great that you keep your mind open for creative opportunities," Daniel said. "Your work just keeps getting better and better..."

"You are three for three tonight, batting a thousand, my man," Ed said. "I'm envious."

"Billy Collins would be impressed," I added.

"That bald drummer dude?" Ish asked.

"I believe you're thinking of *Phil* Collins," I said, "but he would be impressed, as well. Billy Collins, in my opinion, might be one the most creative poets... ever."

"One clever dude for sure," Daniel said. "He was the Poet Laureate several years back."

"Laureate? Like the cowboys use?" Ish asked.

Wayne shook his head in disbelief, but refrained from commenting on Ish's ignorance.

"I believe you are confusing *laureate* with *lariat*," Matty corrected. "The Poet Laureate is an honor bestowed upon a person who has achieved distinction in the field of poetry. I think they hold the title for one year."

"Oh, well thanks for clarifyin', college boy," Ish said with sarcasm.

"Leon, do you ever share your poems with your students?" Ed asked.

"Funny you should ask. Normally I do not, but because this one had a History spin on it, I read it to my last period class."

"What was their reaction? Were they impressed?"

"Actually, I did not get much of a reaction at all. Some mumbled that they liked it; some looked at me as if I was losing it. It was a little disappointing, but it was the last period of the day, the room was warm, they were all wiped out."

"That's too bad." Ed said. "Read it to your first period, soon as class starts. I bet they'll love it."

"I think Ed's right, Leon," I said. "Plus, the kids will get to see a different side of you. It might very well inspire some of your students who are reluctant writers."

"Thanks for the feedback, guys. Definitely food for thought."

"Daniel, would you please go next?" I asked.

"I'll go, but I need to apologize ahead of time. My poem is not as fun, as creative, or as amusing as Leon's."

"Life would be dull without different perspectives," I said. "We've enjoyed your other work; I'm sure we'll appreciate this one as well."

We Cast Long Shadows

from which we cannot escape
no matter where we turn
those shadows are there
not to haunt
but to remind us
that when we step into
the light
there will always be
a silhouette, a dark, yet
transparent outline
a representation,
a proof of our being
that lengthens
like our past
as the sun sets
upon us

•   •   •   •   •

"Some people cast *wide* shadows," Ish carefully mumbled out of the side of his mouth.

"That's a cool poem, Daniel... but... but... "Matty stammered, "and I mean this respectfully... it's..."

Wayne took over, "Introspective... and *brief*. I love it."

"Yeah, something like that," Matty said. "The photograph really works, as well."

"Thanks. I have been looking forward for an opportunity to play with chiaroscuro."

"Ain't that against the law?" Ish asked.

"Chiaroscuro, is that the brand of camera you use?" Matty asked.

"No, I'm sorry; I should have just said shadow and light. Chiaroscuro is a Renaissance art term. Chiro, or light, and *oscuro* for dark. Many of the images we have captured so far have had elements of it. You would be familiar with the master painters that were famous for Chiaroscuro. Da Vinci, Rembrandt, and one of my favorites, Vermeer."

"The pearl earring dude?" Matty asked.

"Yep, the pearl earring dude."

"That girl was a babe," Matty said with a grin.

"In the painting or in the movie?"

"Both."

We laughed at Matty and his youthful enthusiasm and innocence. Ed's face got a little serious as he addressed Daniel.

"Your poems seem to have an edge of sadness about them. I'm just curious... do you feel better after writing them... or sadder?"

"The poem came out more philosophical and... gloomier than I had intended," Daniel said. "I spend quite a bit of time alone... usually by choice. Being reflective or introspective happens when you don't have a lot of distractions. I'll admit this group has been my favorite distraction."

Daniel did not really answer Ed's question, but Ed didn't push the issue.

"I can relate to your thoughts on solitude," Ed said. "But honestly, it's taken me quite a bit of time to get accustomed to, and to appreciate it. I like the poem a lot Daniel."

"You almost sound apologetic," I said to Daniel. "And you needn't be. The piece works. Thanks for sharing."

"Glad to do it. I was just curious fellas... and I need you to be completely honest with me," Daniel said, followed by a serious pause. "Does the shadow in the picture... make my butt look fat?"

The group was amused at the question coming from the big man and at his deadpan delivery.

"Was that your shadow?" Leon asked. "No offense but the shadow makes you look *thinner*."

"No it's not me; it's a guy I work with. It was too difficult to take a picture of my own shadow, because it just wouldn't cooperate... I was forced to let it go."

"Now that you mention it," Leon said, "I thought I saw a shadow in the unemployment line."

"Maybe it could job shadow with Ish or Matty," Ed suggested with a straight face.

"I works better alone, I ain't inta people shadowin' me," Ish said.

"But, are you okay with shadows peopling you?" Matty asked.

"Y'all are weird," Ish said with a dismissive wave of his hand.

"Well, now that that's settled," I said. "Ed, could you please present next?"

"Sure. I did like you said and went to one of my favorite places, and the poem just came to me. I rushed home, grabbed my notebook, and started writing."

Winter Wheat

The winter wheat is nearing harvest.
I've watched it burst through the topsoil in perfect green rows.
Watched it pull inch by inch towards a summer sky,
watched the green slip away and give way to tan.

Soon the combine will come through, then the bailer
leaving a vast, dusty-blonde crew cut.
Until that day, I'll enjoy the ballet.
Every day the same cast but a different show.

The heads, bearded spikes, are fanned out and drying.
Looking like upright paddles but acting like sails,
they dance their hypnotic sway as the wind picks up.
Starting from the west, a wave of golden-yellow grain rolls, a limber ocean
gathering speed...

No longer am I on a tractor by the edge of my neighbor's field.
I'm on the salt-stained deck of the Pequod
grabbing the harpoon from the hands of Queequeg.
Starbuck opens his mouth to protest but thinks better of it.

RICK THORPE

I raise the mighty spear above my head as I spy the beast
wait... wait... wait till he breaks the surface...

It's not the whale but the shadow of a cloud.
I look up to the sky, see the makings of a mid-day storm,
throw the tractor in gear, and head to the house for lunch.

•　　•　　•　　•　　•

"Another winner," Leon said to Ed. "I think you were born to be a man who works in, and observes the outdoors."

"And to write about it," Daniel added.

"Thanks, fellas... I appreciate that."

"Not only a good poem and picture," Matty said. "He threw in some fantastic *Moby Dick* references."

"Ha Ha, and only Ishmael survives, bitches!" Ish bellowed.

"You read the book!" Matty shouted. "What did you think?"

"That ol' Gregory Peck was a nut job."

"C'mon, Ish! Gregory Peck was the guy who played Ahab in the *movie*," Leon said. "You didn't read the book did you?"

"That book was too damned long! I saw the movie at the library and they let me watch it right there. Hooked me up with a player and some headphones. Had me a good ol' time... only thing missin' was the popcorn."

"I bet you asked for some, didn't ya?" Daniel asked.

"Damn straight I did... They laughed at me...thought I was kiddin'."

"That's a bummer, Ish. Some people just don't get it," Ed said.

"I hear ya."

"Back to Ed's poem," I said. "Outstanding job. I thought this assignment would be right up your alley. You had a slight advantage over the other guys."

"That's true. You know, I should have you gentlemen... and Ish, out to the farm sometime. It would be fun to show you all around."

"I'm all for it," I said. "What do you think guys?"

"I'm in," Daniel said without hesitation.

"Wouldn't miss the opportunity," Leon said.

"You bet," Matty said with a big grin. "But I'd have to catch a ride with someone."

"I got ya covered kid," Ish said with a nod and a wink.

"You up to date on your shots?" Daniel asked Matty.

"I believe so."

"Wayne, you up for it?" I asked.

"Can we wait until the pollen count is down?"

"Sure," Ed said.

"Sounds like a plan," I said. "Ish, could you please share next?"

"You got it, chief. Now I will warn y'all this is a freakin' long one. Daniel here came up with the title. He said it sounded like an epic adventure, something *Homer* like. Personally I don't recall the Simpsons havin' a situation like this... but, then again, I ain't seen every episode. I trust Daniel so I went with it."

"Daniel, I'm sure Ish appreciates your help," I said. "I'm a big believer in collaboration. If you are ever too busy to help him, or you need help yourself, please let me know. That goes for anyone here. Anything you want to add before we see his poem?"

"This is a little different than his other pieces," Daniel said. "It's crass and inappropriate... but then again... so is Ish. He came to the bar after quite an adventure in the great outdoors. I told him, 'That's your poem!' He was skeptical, but I eventually talked him into it. Like his other work, I decided to keep it as much in his voice as possible. I had him retell me the tale and I recorded it. I then took it and just broke it into paragraphs to represent stanzas with *very* little editing. Needless to say, it was a grammatical and spell-check nightmare. It reads more like a short story than a poem, but oh well. He sat with me and was completely involved in the writing and editing process. He'll be ready to fly on his own soon."

Ishmael's Odyssey

I've never been in a Metro park, man it's a big ass place. A fella could get lost pretty damn easy. It's weird to see trees so big and without tacked on advertisements and wads of gum. I saw a squirrel the size of a house cat, come to think of it, maybe it was a house cat. I was starting to like nature... until nature called. That's right... I had to go and bad, and I'm to blame! I shoulda never had that microwave burrito for breakfast, one I had found under my car seat.

My gut is howling like a muffled Basset Hound, when, to my great relief, I spot a restroom up ahead. It appeared to be about a hundred yards away. I'm not partial to running, but I broke into a trot. I reach the place bent over. Jogging, I have discovered, does not aid in holding in one's bowels. Greeting me on the door is a sign readin' 'Closed for Repairs, use the North Entrance'. I got news for the idiot who put up this here sign... *My South* end won't make it to *your* North end!

In addition to being doubled over I've also broken into a sweat and starting to panic. Then it hits me! Not an accident, an idea! It's forty percent inspiration, seventy percent desperation. I spied me a post with a sign that says, 'Keep our Metro park clean. Please curb your dog.' Not sure what 'curb' means, but under the sign is a rack of paper bags and a rubber glove dispenser. I grabs me a bag and a couple of rubber gloves and make a bent over dash for the nearest bush.

I'm pretty well hidden but with all these weirdos with cameras on their phones, I can't take chances. I got a reputation to protect and I don't want to end up on no internet. So I pull a glove over my head. It was tighter than hell and it didn't take too long to figure out I couldn't see and nor could I breathe! So I lift the glove up to my eyebrows and rapidly fumble with my belt buckle and unbutton my pants. Fiddlin' around with that dumb ass glove wasted me some valuable time, what was I thinkin'!?

With the bag situated 'neath me, I finally am able to relax knowing relief is only seconds away. I hit my target, for the most part, and let out a particular sigh that I usually save for other occasions. So there I am with my pants around my ankles, wishin' I had a smoke, when I hear a rustlin' sound. The rustlin' gets louder and closer when suddenly a little dog pops out of the bushes right next to me. The damn thing nearly scared the shit outa' me, but it was too late for that. Least he weren't a skunk.

Ol' panic returns when I realize this mutt has got an owner out there lookin' for him somewhere. Well, sure enough that little rat started yippin' and yappin' and gave away our location to the owner. She was a skinny, spiky-haired woman in yoga pants. I push the dog through the bushes I am thinkin' she will be so relieved to find her precious pooch she will not spy me still in a squat. She snaps him up and turns. I know I'm not outta the woods yet, both figuratively and literally.

The lady has the little dog under her arm like a football and is headin' for the end zone. I'm free! Well, not so fast… my gut gives one last dying rumble loud 'nuff to shake the acorns off the maples. She whips around and sees me. Her free hand goes up to cover her mouth, stiflin' a holler. I scramble to pull up my drawers as quick as I can, but in my mad haste I stumble and fall forward.

As luck would have it, the spiky-haired lady has run straight to a park ranger who has just pulled up.

She's pointin' towards me with the hand holdin' the dog and pinching her nose shut with the other. Now this don't make a licka' sense seein' as how she's probably fifty yards away at this point. The ranger comes a runnin' with his gun drawn, like I'm some kinda crazed felon or somethin'. He closes in on me as I scamper to my feet. I holler, "Don't shoot officer it was an emergency!" "It was an emergency to flash that poor woman? Put your hands where I can see them, pervert!"

"Look officer, I ain't no flasher! I had to go really bad! Could you not wave that gun at my manparts?" "What kind of weirdo, with a rubber glove on his head, relieves himself in a public park?" "What kinda weirdo holds a gun on a man and won't let him pull up his drawers?" "Come with me and we'll get to the bottom of this mess. Speaking of *mess*, bring that bag with you." I mumbles, "We woulda not had this mess had you picked up a *plunger* instead of that there pistol."

• • • • •

"I'm moved to tears," Leon said to Ish. "What an adventure. Was the little dog a Shih Tzu? Did everything come out all right?"

"Nice pun," Matty said. "Yeah Ish, you left us hangin'. What happened?"

"Ol' Barney Fife gave me a freakin' ticket! A hundred and fifty bucks!"

"He soiled your good name," Leon said. "Defamation of character."

"And *defecation* of character," Matty added.

"Exactly!" Ish shouted.

As usual, Wayne had a sour look of disapproval and let out a heavy sigh.

"Disgusting and wrong on many different levels," he said.

"Now this whole time are you still wearing the rubber glove on your head like a giant chicken?" Leon asked.

"Yeah, I forgot about it till I got back to my car."

"So your crime was *fouling* up the park? Matty quipped.

"I thought I already made that clear," Ish said with a hint of irritation.

"Good one, Matty," Leon said. "You're in the zone."

"You shoulda' flown the coop," Matty suggested to Ish.

"Naw, he had me dead to rights," Ish said with a sniff.

"Quit while you're ahead, Matty," Leon said. "It's only a matter of time before you lay an egg."

"Sorry," Matty said. "Hope I didn't ruffle anyone's feathers... that's my last one, I promise."

"Don't give up your day jobs, fellas," Daniel said with a grin.

"That story could have only happened to you, Ish," Ed said. "What did you do with the bag? I really hope you didn't throw it out your car window on the way home."

"Nah, only a jerk would do somethin' like that. I put it in the bed of the ranger's pickup truck when he was writin' out the ticket."

"How could you do such a thing?" Wayne asked incredulously.

"What was I 'posed ta do, *Dewayne*... let it ride shotgun home with me? Talk about disgusting!"

"Bro," Matty said, "I wouldn't go back to that park... *ever*... that dude is gonna be pissed!"

"Don't plan on goin' back... had my filla nature."

"Entertaining, Ish," I said. "Not sure this is what my dad had in mind…"

"It's my fault. I apologize," Daniel said. "I couldn't pass up the chance to help Ish document that epic tale."

"No worries. I agree that tale is too…uh… *interesting*… to pass up. Matty, could you present next?"

"Yep. Just a forewarning, mine is not very entertaining. Here goes."

Dawn Can Wait

Lying in a sleepy meadow
of Indian grass and wildflowers
they watch a wispy gray cloud
slide past
the thin sliver
of an August moon.
Restless leaves above
pause and strain to hear
their whispered dreams.

Hands search and find,
fingers entwine,
eyes close,
breath and time slow,
dawn can wait.

·   ·   ·   ·   ·

Wayne stood up... with some effort... and started clapping his hands.

"Bravo! Very romantic... well done, young sir."

Matty nodded his head without speaking. He seemed a little embarrassed by the exuberant praise. The rest of the men stared at Wayne, so he sat down.

"Another good one kid," Leon said. "Was that written from experience or wishful thinking?"

"Unfortunately, wishful thinking. I was sitting on top of this hill near a tree just taking in the quiet. These clouds started rolling past and they were spectacular. I've never told anyone this before, but I'm a bit of a freak about clouds, always have been. And I was thinking it would be nice to share this moment with somebody."

"You're inta *clouds*?" Ish asked with a perplexed look on his face.

"I know it's weird. Many people like a pure blue sky, but not me. When clouds start to roll in, I'm..."

"On cloud nine?" Leon asked.

"Yes... Funny, but true."

"That's not that odd, kid," Daniel said. "There was an English painter, John Constable, famed for his landscapes *especially* clouds. Lots of people are really into clouds."

"I must admit," Wayne confessed. "I would be one of those people. My wife thought it was silly, and then she became addicted to them as well."

"Seriously? I thought I was in the minority."

"Heck, there's even a Cloud Appreciation Society," Daniel said. "You guys should join."

Matty had a very skeptical look on his face.

"C'mon man. A society... for people... who appreciate... *clouds*?"

"Some folks join groups just so's they can belong somewhere," Ish said quietly.

There was a stretch of silence. The comment was definitely food for thought, but the fact that it came from Ish, made the reason to pause twofold. Leon pointed his finger at Daniel, and broke the silence.

"Dude, you sure know a lot of stuff. I know you said you read a great deal, but so do I... but I don't know anything about some of the stuff you bring up."

"I'm just curious about things I guess."

"I think it's cool," Ed said with a grin. "I'm envious."

"I think what Leon is stumped by is; 'How can a guy who works in a bar, and looks like I do, be somewhat of an intellectual'. Am I right?"

Leon had a worried, concerned look on his face.

"I'm sorry... I didn't mean to offend you..."

"No, No, please don't worry about it. I'm not offended. I get it. But it's... complicated..."

A wave of relief appeared to wash over Leon... over all of us.

"And let me add," Daniel said. "It never was my intention to come across as a 'know-it-all'."

"I think I can speak for everyone," I said. "We really appreciate what you bring to our conversations. I personally am learning a lot... from *all* of you."

"Amen to that," Ish said. "Hell, I don't even know what the big man is sayin' half the time, but I still 'preciate it."

"That means a lot comin' from you, Ish," Daniel deadpanned.

"I got your back, brother."

"Can we get back to the kid's poem?" Daniel asked.

"Wonderful idea," Wayne said. "If the young man is going to lie in the grass with a lady friend, he should go to the drug store first... and buy a good over-the-counter antihistamine."

Not the advice I thought was coming, but, then again, not really that surprising.

"And while you're at the drug store get yourself... a can of *OFF*. Nothin' can ruin a romantic evenin' like a swarm of skeeters."

Ditto.

"Uh... good advice gentleman," Matty said. "I'll take it under consideration."

"Get off your ass, kid," Leon said. "Introduce yourself to that girl you're hot for. After you get to know each other better, ask her to watch clouds with you in that field. Read her some of your poems; she would be flattered."

"You should do it, Matty," Daniel said with a nod.

"I concur," Wayne said. "Woo her with your words and charm."

"Great advice coming from a bunch of single guys. I'm still not sure how to even approach her or what to say."

"I'll quote Jack Kerouac," Leon said. "'One day I will find the words, and they will be simple'."

"I think you oughtta invite her to one of your modelin' gigs," Ish said with his patented smirk.

"So my intro line would go something like this, 'Pardon me, Ma'am. You don't know me... but would you like to see me in the nude?' That sound about right?"

"I've used that exact line often," Ish said. "Works about half the time."

"Let me guess," Ed said. "The other half results in either a slap in the face or a knee to the crotch?"

"Yep, sometimes both the slap *and* the knee."

"As much as I love this conversation," I said. "I think we should move on to Wayne's poem before we run out of time tonight. Wayne, I know you are not a fan of the outdoors. Were you able to go outside and get inspired?"

"Oh contraire. I love the outdoors, that is, when I'm heavily lathered with a layer of industrial strength SPF 50. As I said last week, I just cannot really venture out too much when the pollen count is high. And yes, I was able to write my poem."

"What did ya do, Dewayne... stick your head out the winda?" Ish asked.

"No Ishmael, I did not stick my head out of a *winda*... I went to a park, as you did, on my lunch hour... Thank heavens I was not there at the same time as you. My poem is a little mean and snarky, but I was extremely irritated with my girlfriend... I asked her to accompany me to the park and she claimed she was too busy... again. Therefore, this poem is the venting of my frustrations. I'm over it now, but I didn't have time to write another one."

A Summer's Day

Shall I compare thee to a summer's day?
I shall

In the high, billowy clouds, I see your face...
puffy and white

With the afternoon wind, I feel your breath...
thick, oppressive, and hot

The presence of the bright yellow sun... like your presence,
makes me break into a sweat

The fragrance of the wildflowers... like your fragrance,
makes my eyes water

The swift-moving brook tumbling over the rocks...
like you, my dear, rambles on, and on, and on...

• • • • •

"Brother, that is harsh," Leon said. "Funny as hell... but harsh. You're a modern-day Bard."

"Modern day *what*?" Ish asked.

"In medieval times a bard was a poet or a storyteller. 'The Bard' was a nickname for William Shakespeare," Leon explained. "Wayne's poem is a spoof on a Shakespeare sonnet."

"Nice job *Bard*-ass," Ish quietly mumbled.

"You plan on giving your girl that poem?" Ed asked with a laugh.

"Are you kidding me? My large, alabaster keister would be out on the street in a heartbeat. I plan on destroying all copies of this as soon as we dismiss tonight."

"I bet it felt good to vent like that," Matty said.

"It really did. I felt all this bottled-up frustration with her and needed an outlet."

"Is this the same girl you got roses for?" Daniel asked. "I'm by no means an expert, but it sounds like your relationship is kind of rocky."

"Who says that poem was written by me? Those poems from last week were to be anonymous."

"Even *I* figured out ya wrote that one, Dewayne," Ish said.

"I really do like her, and I've tried many ways to woo her, but it always seems to backfire."

Wayne might be the only man I've ever met to consistently use the word, 'woo'.

"Would ya like my advice, Dewayne?" Ish asked.

"It's *Wayne,* damn it... and no thank you."

"Maybe you're trying too hard," Ed offered.

"Perhaps you're right. I just do *not* want to lose her... I think she might be the one."

"Don't ya mean the *two*?" Ish asked. "Weren't ya married once before?"

"A *huge* mistake."

"Big gal was she?" Ish asked.

"Well... let's just say we were a good fit... physically."

"Say no more... *please*," Ish said with a grimace.

"It's really getting late guys," I said. "You need to be given your next assignment before we dismiss for the evening. I would like the next poem to be from the vantage point of your vehicle. What you see out your window or windshield. I know it sounds odd... but trust me on this. Same rules apply... real, imagined, humorous, inspired... whatever works. Good luck and see you next week."

"Before we go," Ed said. "I would love to see a poem from Leon, written from the perspective of a *student* in that nude drawing class."

"Quite a daunting task..." Leon said, rubbing his chin. "But, I accept your challenge."

"*Great*... can't wait to see what he conjures up this time," Matty said with more than a hint sarcasm."

"Don't leave poor Matty hangin'," Daniel said. "So to speak."

"Alright," I said, "next week should be as entertaining as this week. See ya."

That went well. I was worried about the men not doing the assignments or doing them half-assed. Not only were they making a strong effort, but now I have guys doing extra work. You can't beat that. This week's assignment is a little offbeat; I hope they can rise to the challenge.

Ish really needs to back off the needling towards Wayne. My scolding didn't really sink in a great deal. The other men are hesitating to intervene, perhaps for fear of confrontation. I think they are waiting for Wayne to stand up for himself. I might have to pull Ish to the side before this comes to a head.

WEEK FIVE

I was late arriving and all of the men were sitting around talking while waiting for me. For the most part, they seem to enjoy each other's company. I would not have guessed that when I first met them. Some of the men are still a mystery to me but I look forward every week to reading their poems, seeing their photographs, and to listening to their conversations.

"Sorry I'm late guys. I hope everyone had a productive week. Leon, any luck with Ed's challenge?"

"Actually it was easier and more fun than I thought it would be. I even tickled myself with my artwork. It kinda works better if you look at both poems side by side, but here goes."

Musing during my first art class

The Human Form 101... I wish they would have added, *With Khakis"*
Nude guy in front of me, no cover charge nor three drink minimum... nice
I wonder if he is part Asian...
He bears a striking resemblance to my Philosophy T.A....
That has to be the widest ass I have ever seen...
That was a typo, I meant, that has to be the *whitest* ass I've ever seen...'
Is it possible to have a typo in your thoughts? I guess it would be a 'thinko'...
Cute guy in spite of his *short*comings... could use a little work on his core...
We have been here for half an hour and the lady to my right has yet to put
pencil to paper...... same with the guy to my left'
That is the oddest pose, ever... is he looking for car keys under some bushes?
Thank God we're not working in clay...
...exfoliate, exfoliate, exfoliate...
That reminds me, I need to call the pet groomer...
I swear I smell coconut oil...

I wonder if he's okay... the occasional grimace is worrisome...
Wow! He really needs to get *that* looked at...
How odd, that's the third time the custodian has emptied that trash can...
This is the last time I sit in the third row...
'Is it my imagination or does he keep looking this way... Oh my!

•   •   •   •   •

"Wow, you did it!" Ed said. "As good as or better than the first one. I would bow down before you, but these old knees are about shot."

"I'm speechless," I said.

"I, too, am without speech," Daniel said.

"As much as it pains me to be the butt of the joke," Matty said, "that was as funny as the first one. And you're right, it works better when you see both poems side by side."

"Great sketch of the kid," Ish said.

"The likeness is uncanny," Wayne said, "but you should have added his curly locks."

"You captured his sinewy grace and regal bearing," Daniel deadpanned.

"Thanks for putting me in a Pittsburgh Pirates hat," Matty said with a grin, "and covering my genitals with a pencil. Nice touch."

"A pencil could probably cover 'em in real life as well," Ish said, with of course... a smirk.

"Okay... quickly moving on," I said. "I agree with the others, Leon, great use of humor. You have a quirky style, but it really works. Okay, anybody ready to present?"

"Since the spotlight, as well as the pencil, is on me," Matty said. "I might as well go first. I don't own a car so mine was inspired while riding a city bus, thus the title."

Riding in the Back of a City Bus

Staring out the window
sliding past a sea of
cars, shops, and nameless pedestrians
focusing on none of them
My mind working and reworking
the elusive first line of a poem
almost have it then gone again
slipping through my fingers
like a bar of wet soap
Finally, in my grasp, I have it
Not wanting to risk it to memory
I rifle through my book bag
looking for my notebook and pen
that are sitting, useless,
on an unmade bed miles away
Using the grime and condensation
that coat the window
I write down the line with my finger

RICK THORPE

Silently I repeat it over and over
hoping to burn it into my memory
Getting off at my stop
I turn back and watch
the backward image of the line pull away
Wondering, how long will it last there
Will it be read?
Appreciated?
Added to?
Or will it vanish with one swipe
of a dirty sleeve?

•   •   •   •   •

"Great job, Matty," Leon said. "Interesting concept there, and I'm sure this has probably already been done, but what if you intentionally left a starter line for a poem out in public and invited others to add a line. As long as you didn't end that first line with Nantucket, it would be cool to see what the end result would be."

"I love the poem kid," Daniel said. "You have a unique voice as a writer. I have a question though; did you really leave your notebook at home?"

"No, I rarely leave home without it... If I did, I could use my laptop or phone. I wrote my initials in the bus window, that's when the idea of the poem came to me."

"It's clever," Ed said. "I really like it."

"I agree, well done," I said. "Who's next?"

"I'll go," Daniel said. "Be prepared, I've channeled my inner Leon."

G'day Mate

I had just spent five bucks at the car wash
and pulled out into the noonday traffic
when a bird shits on my windshield
right in front of my face.

The splatter is the size of a dinner plate
I'm wondering if it was not a bird,
but a pterodactyl.

I'm just about to hit the wash and wipers
when my anger and frustration
turns to amazement.

I notice that the mess looks exactly like
the Continent of Australia.
On closer inspection
I see the island state of Tasmania,

The Sydney Opera House and
a faint outline of the Great Barrier Reef.

Pulling me out of my trance
is an odd noise, a humming.
Turning the knobs on the broken radio
and banging on the cracked dashboard
do nothing to diminish the buzz.

I lean in closer with a tilted ear.
It's the faint sound of a didgeridoo...
It's the last thing I remember
before smashing into
the car in front of me.

•   •   •   •   •

"Wow," Ed said. "That started out odd and just... got odder... I love it... You've got a rival, Leon."

"I'm proud of my young, very large Jedi," Leon said.

"You guys are a trip," Matty said. "The poem is fantastic, but I have a random question about the bottom photograph. How did you create that mess on the windshield?"

"A map of Australia and 5 packs of Arby's horseradish sauce."

"You sure that's Australia?" Ish asked with a puzzled look. "It looks to me like Ohio taking a shit on... I'm not sure, but by the angle of that little blob, I'm guessin' West Virginia. Which I resent... I gots kinfolk there."

"Kinfolk on that windshield or in West Virginia?" Leon asked.

"Real funny, teacher boy."

"That 'little blob'," Daniel said with a laugh, "is supposed to be New Zealand."

"Whatever you say, big boy," Ish said with a grin and a dismissive wave of his hand. "And, by the way, I'll take some of the credit for that poem, boys... that was my car he was drivin'. It was my turn to help ol' Daniel out, 'steada the other ways 'round."

"That so Daniel?" Ed asked. "That explains the hula girl on the dash."

"It's true. Ish knew I didn't have a car, so he loaned me his so I could complete the assignment."

"I'm sorry to have made this difficult on you guys who don't have a car." I said. "And, I gotta ask, how did you get inspired to write that tale?"

"To show my gratitude, and because my 4X biohazard suit was at the cleaners, I took his LTD to the car wash. A place, I assumed, it had never been before..."

"Low and behold, that car was yella... not gray!" Ish interjected with a shout.

Daniel continued, "...then sure enough a bird relieves himself on the window while I'm pulling out. I'm thinking well that's Murphy's Law in action. In reality, I wasn't mad. I was amused by the irony. So anyway, I come to a stop sign and put on the brakes. Ish neglected to tell me his brakes are slow to work when the car gets wet, so I lightly tap into the dude in front of me. Not really even a fender bender, but I get out to check and to apologize. I walk up to the guy's car door; he looks at me wide-eyed, locks the door and then takes off."

"Scared him, did ya?" Ed asked.

"It's a gift," Daniel said with a modest shrug.

"I bet he thought you were going to pull him right out of that car," Leon said.

"I woulda thought the same thing if I saw you coming at me," Matty said. "I would have soiled more than just a windshield."

"Yeah," Daniel said with a shake of his head, "but I was clearly at fault, the guy didn't *back* into me... if you potentially damage someone's property you should at least check to make sure, and like I said, to apologize."

"It's alright, Daniel, I won't charge ya none for smashing up my car," Ish said smugly.

"Thanks Ish, you're a real pal."

"Sounds like your parents raised you right, Daniel," Ed said.

"My mother was a good person and taught us early on between right and wrong, but she died when I was young. My ol' man, on the other hand, would steal the shoes off your feet. I tried to honor her, best I could, by doing the right thing. My brothers, on the other hand, took more after my dad."

"Well, that was a good piece of writing," I said. "Who would like to go next?"

"Here's mine," Ish volunteered.

Jump Start

So they say texting and driving is dangerous, not a worry when you're phoneless.
Have you tried writing a poem while driving? Ain't no walk in the park my friend.
I borrowed my sister's piece o' crap car 'cause my friend Daniel was usin' my Ford LTD.
It starts to get dark so I pull into a parking lot and turn on the dome light so I can see.
Two freakin' hours, four broke pencils, thirty wads of paper, and a liter of RC Cola later,
I decide to move on and try my luck again tomorrow.

As is par for the course, when I turn the key, this pile o' junk won't start.
I weren't here that long but the dome light musta drained the battery.
Why would ya loan somebody, especially your brother, a car with a weak battery?
I get out, slam the door, and flag down a suit in a Volvo and ask for a jump.
He looks at me then sneaks a glance at my sister's funky-ass station wagon, and hesitates.

I'm thinkin' 'What the hell dude, me and the car ain't gonna give you the ebola virus!'

Well surprise, surprise.... this heap has no freakin' jumper cables!
The dude in the Volvo has some, but he has to put on a pair of leather work gloves first.
Like I got all the time in the world! I'm thinkin', step it up rich boy!
He sees me rollin' my eyes and he mumbles, "ingrate." Whatever that means.

I finally get the jump and nod to the suit to let him know that my engine turned over.
He gets out of the Volvo and walks around to unhook the cables from his battery.
For a moment his view of me is blocked by my uplifted hood.
When he gets to the grill of the car, he finds me sprawled out on the ground.
I'm floppin' around, eyes rolled back in my head, tongue a stickin' out.
Jumper cables clamped to the seat of my Carharts, one to each ass cheek.

He screams like a freakin' school girl and drops the cables.
My convulsions of mock shock convert to convulsions of laughter.
The suit throws down his gloves, spins on his fancy loafers and stomps back to his car.
I'm still lyin' on the ground when he peels out, sprayin' me with fine bits of asphalt.
Out of the Volvo's window shoots a well-manicured middle finger.
The word "Psycho" pierces the night air as the suit speeds away.
I nod my head in agreement, pick up the jumper cables and the gloves.
I love free shit.

•   •   •   •   •

The men laughed -with the exception of Wayne- throughout the reading of the poem and for a solid minute afterward.

"Ish, have you noticed you have a common theme with most of your poems?" Leon asked.

"And what would that be?"

"Confrontation."

"It does seem ta find me."

"The question is... do you enjoy it?" Daniel asked.

"Why would I enjoy gettin' myself in a jam?"

"Some people find it a rush to get into a fight or flight situation," Daniel said.

"Like an adrenaline junkie," Ed said. "As a cop I saw it all the time."

"Probably saw it in other cops too."

"Sure, I saw a few. Guys like that were dangerous to be partners with."

"There a pill of some sorts I can takes for it?" Ish asked no one in particular.

"I bet some sessions with my dad would have helped you," I said. "I'm sure I could hook you up with one of his colleagues, if you're interested."

"Whataya think, Daniel?" Ish asked.

"I think it might help you to become a better person, and ultimately that is what everyone's goal should be. You have potential; you don't want to go around being a dickhead your whole life."

"Amen," Wayne mumbled.

"So what is your degree in, Daniel... Psychology or Philosophy?" Leon asked.

"Art History."

"I knew it!" Leon said. "You been holdin' back on us!"

"I wasn't holding back," Daniel said calmly. "If I tell you I have a degree yet work as a bouncer, it leads to a bunch of questions that I didn't want to answer."

"Fair enough... no questions," Leon said with his hands in the air.

"Cool... thank you," Daniel said. "Let's move on."

"I'm ready," Wayne said. "Let me explain mine first. I drove down a road I often take to work and I was reminded of an experience I had on that same stretch of road this past winter. The picture will throw you at first, or make you hungry, but please be patient. I hope you enjoy it."

The Ditch

My car creeps along through the monstrous storm,
the steering wheel gripped tight with knuckles as white
as the snow that swirls about me.

In the distance, I can barely make out
what appears to be
your vehicle in the ditch.

My heart begins to race with fear and anticipation
Fear...... if it's you, are you okay?
Anticipation.... if it's you, this is my chance to be
your knight in a shining Toyota.

I gently tap the brakes and slow to a stop
alongside what might be your SUV.

RICK THORPE

I ease down the window to get a better view
of who is in the stranded car.

The driver does the same.
I can see that it is an elderly woman.
She resembles my Aunt Blanche.
Her hair is as white as... I would say snow
but I already used that comparison in the first stanza.

Through the roaring wind I mouth the words,
"Are you okay?"
She nods yes.
I notice her small chin is quivering.

I give her a 'thumbs up' signal as I pull away.
I glance at my watch.
I hope I'm not late for work;
it's Friday so there will be
doughnuts in the breakroom.
I hope there are ones with sprinkles...
I love sprinkles...
Hmmm... sprinkles

•   •   •   •   •

Once again, the men laughed long after the poem was finished being read. This seemed to please Wayne. He actually had a small smile on his face... but the smile only lasted for about a second or two.

"'Magine that," Ish said with a lopsided grin, "Wayne choosin' a doughnut over a woman!"

"Brother, that is really funny," Matty said with a laugh. "And that is one big-ass doughnut!"

"I can honestly say I stopped at just one," Wayne said without expression.

"You didn't really leave an old lady stranded in a ditch did you?"

"That would be cold," Matty added.

"Literally and figuratively," Leon said.

"I pride myself on being a gentleman," Wayne said, his head held high. "I called a tow truck and waited for it to arrive. I thought the poem would be more interesting if the hero turned out to be a heel."

"I think you're right," I said. "It works. It comes as a complete surprise."

"I think Leon has yet *another* rival when it comes to humor," Ed said.

Leon hardened his face, squinted his eyes, and gave us a decent Clint Eastwood impersonation.

"Bring it on."

"What do you have for us Leon?" I asked.

"Well, I have a small issue with road rage. My kids are always on my ass about it, so sure enough, I caught myself getting pissed-off about some idiot's driving this week, and it dawned on me, this is what my topic should be."

Losing my Temper

I lost my temper last night, then I found him sitting by the side of the road.
I pulled over and opened the passenger side door for him.
"Hop in," I said through the cloud of dust I had just created.
He coughed, brushed himself off, and got in without saying a word.
"Look, I'm really sorry about last night," I said.
Temper didn't answer me for the longest time.
He just stared out the window, lost in thought.
Finally, he cleared his throat and said,
"You know life is much better when you keep me."
"I know, I know..."
Dude, I'm not sure you *do* know! A couple of times you nearly got us killed!"
"Isn't that a bit of an exaggeration?"
"How about the time you got into a fight with a bouncer because he spilled your beer?"
"It was an import!"
"How about the time you screamed at that couple who cut in front of you at

the movies?"

"Yeah, I remember that; I lost you *and* a tooth."

"You found me in a half-eaten tub of popcorn...and it was stale."

"Sorry man..."

"I have two more words for you.... road rage."

"You have a point..."

"And think about the relationships you've ruined."

"Too many to count. You're right, what can I do?"

He put his hand on my shoulder. I knew he was looking at me, but I kept my eyes on the road. Then he said softly,

"Next time you get angry and you think you are about to lose me..."

He paused to formulate the right words.

"Yes?" I said with just a hint of impatience.

"Next time you are about to lose me, grab my hand and squeeze."

"Okay, and then what?"

"And then hold on tight till the anger and frustration pass."

"That simple?"

"Easier said than done. It will be tough but it will be okay to let go."

"Like when?"

"Like when you see someone being abused or taken advantage of."

"Then it will be okay to lose you?"

"Let's just say I'll understand."

I smiled and gave an approving nod. After a bit I said, "Thanks for not giving up on me."

"It's all good, man," he said as he flipped his Ray Bans on. "We need to work as a team."

At that moment a rusty Crown Vic cut in front of me, missing my front bumper by inches. My right hand rose out of instinct, ready to slam down on the horn... but I hesitated.

My passenger shouted, "What are you waiting for? Let him have it!"

"Temper, Temper."

"My bad," he said. We both burst out laughing.

I pulled up alongside the Crown Vic and smiled at the driver.

Temper gave the driver the finger when he thought I wasn't looking.

"Hypocrite," I said, then smashed my palm onto the horn.

· · · · ·

The men did not break out in laughter like they did with some of the other poems but they were clearly amused.

"Clever as hell," Matty said.

"Your mind works different, doesn't it?" Ed asked.

"Had me a Crown Vic once," Ish said randomly to no one in particular.

"Wonderful use of personification, Leon," Wayne said.

"You're getting good at this stuff," Daniel added.

"I agree," I said. "I think you all are."

"Looks like I'm up," Ed said with a grimace. "No pressure or anything."

"I'm sure whatever you came up with will be as good as your previous work," I said. "Let's see what you got."

Stop Light

Stopped at the light on my trip into town
The tic, tic, tic of the truck engine like a
tap, tap on the shoulder, a subtle reminder
that my trusty, rusty companion is a quart low on oil.
I add that quart to my mental errand list.

A school bus pulls up beside me.
I refrain from looking over,
no need to see a smirk and a middle finger.
Out of the corner of the eye, I see a motion.
My curiosity gets the best of me and I glance over.

A young girl with Down's syndrome is waving to me
Blue eyes twinkle behind thick glasses.
She takes a blonde pigtail and puts it under her nose.

RICK THORPE

I smile at the girl with her pretend yellow mustache.
She breaks into a laugh, proud of her joke.

The light changes and as the bus pulls away
the girl blows me a kiss.
I sit for a moment, grinning
my mental errand list no longer seems so
Important.

• • • • •

"Great job, Ed," I said. "We knew you would deliver another good piece."

"You do a nice job of making the ordinary interesting," Daniel said.

"I agree," Leon said, "it's like what a good photographer can do."

"Did anyone else notice that half of our poems this week mention the middle finger?" Matty asked.

"I thought about having the old lady flip me off in my poem," Wayne said.

"Might have been a nice touch," Leon said, scratching his chin in thought. "Piss off a sweet old lady and her true colors come out."

"True," Daniel said. "It would bring out an irony that most of us here love, but it would take away from her innocence and make the reader feel less sorry for her."

"I think we all could have added the middle finger in our poems this week," Matty said. "Daniel could have had that guy flip him off as he sped away. I could have had a passenger, or the bus driver, flip me off as I watched my poem drive off."

"Could have been our theme for tonight," Leon said, "don't you think, George?"

"Might have been autobiographical for some of you," I said.

Right on cue, Ish chimed in.

"I recollect, on average, I get flipped off at least once in a 24-hour period. But, comes to think about it, today's been bird free so far. Guess I ain't agitated anyone yet."

"Don't give up hope," Daniel said, "the night is still young. If you deliver pizzas tonight you will have several opportunities."

The men laughed at that with the exception of Wayne, who stoically nodded his head in agreement.

"Well, we've had another successful week everyone," I said. "You should be proud of your work and feel good about what you are able to create. It's interesting and entertaining. I know we have not discussed our grief and the source of it yet, but I hope the work you have been creating has been somewhat helpful.

Next week's assignment is to give us a snapshot of your life. I know that is broad and vague, but look at it as an opportunity to give us a look at your everyday life, past or present. Could be a monumental moment or an ordinary one. Good luck, and as always, contact me if you need help or advice."

·　　·　　·　　·　　·

The men left and they were all talking with each other, even Wayne and Ish took part, although not with each other. In a rather short period they have somewhat bonded and are becoming friends. It's not anything I'm really doing by a longshot. It's the poetry and the conversation, the comradery. Dad was onto something. It's a shame he's not here to witness it.

WEEK SIX

The men all arrived early and in good spirits. I hope that tonight will be as successful as the past five meetings. I really look forward to these meetings.

"Good evening guys," I said. "It's great to see everyone. I look forward to seeing what you came up with tonight. I realize the topic was not very specific but I was hoping this would bring about more introspection and give you more freedom. Who would like to start us off? Leon, you have taken the lead the last couple of weeks - want to keep up the trend?"

"Sure. Let me set this up a little bit first. A friend of mine that I teach with has been out for a few weeks on paternity leave. We are short on subs, so several of us have been picking up his freshman English classes for him during our planning periods. It's a hassle, but we get paid a little bit to do it and like I said, he is a friend. The idea for this poem came to me when I was daydreaming, looking out the window."

Poets

My students sit, eyes glazed over.
Pulling teeth would be easier than getting them to dissect a poem.
A boy in the front row volunteers his opinion
on the merits of the poem we've just read from the textbook.
I nod my head in agreement, but I don't really hear his monotone remarks.
He knows as well as I, that in reality, this poem is a pile of dung.
I gaze out the window as my thoughts drift like the passing clouds...
'How did this windbag of a poet become so popular in the first place?
Poet Laureate my ass...
If I had just an *ounce* of ambition, I could write circles around this guy!
Women would be wooed.
Grown men would be brought to tears...
Even the straight ones.'

My mind drifts to a classroom in the future...
One of my classic poems has just been recited.
Like a ghost, I float and hover over each desk,
beaming with pride as I read *my* poem and *my* name,

projected on some sort of hologram in front of each student.
Overcome with emotion, I fish through my pockets for a tissue.
A boy in the front row has a question for his teacher about my poem.
However, the teacher does not respond...
He sits at his desk, chin resting in cupped hands...
With faraway-eyes, he stares out the window...

• • • • •

"So they weren't impressed with your Longfellow?" Ish asked with his oft-mentioned smirk. "Now ya knows how Matty feels."

"Funny Ish," Leon replied. "Hurtful, but funny. I guess it was unfortunate for that kid to fall asleep on that page."

"Did you get that young man's permission to take his picture?" Wayne asked with concern.

"Yes, I gently shook him awake and ask him to sign some release papers," Leon said sarcastically. "Heck no, I didn't ask his permission. He shouldn't have fallen asleep."

"Could be a potential lawsuit is all I'm saying."

"That might be okay, force me into an early retirement."

Ish was grinning ear to ear, quietly loving the fact that Wayne was bickering with someone else. Ed finally broke the tension.

"That was another great poem, Leon. Do you ever share these with your fellow teachers? Surely they are as impressed as we are."

"I share with a few close friends. I get a better reaction from my peers than I do my students. They think I should try to publish them or read them at an open mike at some bar."

"You really should," I added in agreement. "Your work is entertaining."

"No doubt," agreed Daniel.

"Actually, I think you all should try to publish," I said, not wanting to slight anyone.

"You're blowin' smoke man," Ish said with a dismissive wave of his hand.

"I'm not," I said, trying not to sound defensive. "I mean it. You gentlemen have come up with some good stuff. Most of it's not ordinary, but that's part of the charm of it. Sure, some of your work has been humorous and quirky, but at times, it's been heartfelt and always interesting."

"Maybe we could compile it all when we are done?" Matty suggested.

"I wouldn't be opposed to that," Leon said

"Nor I," said Wayne.

"If it makes us some dough," Ish said, "I'm all for it."

"Of course we would need to sign some consent forms," Leon said with a hint of sarcasm.

"Indeed," Wayne said with the same hint.

"I'll see what I can do to make it happen," I said. "Who's up next?"

I'll go next," Matty said. "But before I forget, I picked up these bumper stickers from the Art Department, if anybody wants one. They say, 'Art Saves Lives.' I thought Daniel might want one."

"Sure kid I'll take one... even though I don't own a car," Daniel said. "I'll put it up in the bar; try to increase the culture level. Might even stay up on the wall a week or two before some drunk peels it off. Thanks for thinking about me."

"I'll take one for my truck," Ed said. "And one for my brother, Arthur, if you have extras. He would love it."

"Sure thing. Is Arthur an artist?" Matty asked.

"Yes, he is, as a hobby. But more importantly, he's a paramedic."

There was a brief moment of silence before Leon let out a sharp laugh.

"I get it... his name is *Art*... and he saves lives."

"Very clever, Ed." Daniel said with a broad grin.

"Thanks. I think my brother will get a kick out of it. Here is another funny thing. His name is Art Baker and he is into pottery and ceramics. He even has his own kiln."

"So he *bakes* his *art*," Wayne said with a wry smile.

"Never a dull moment around you guys," I said. "Matty, let's see what you got."

"Okay, before I show you this poem.... This situation *never* happened... but it's what I *envision* happening. So please refrain from bombarding me with insults."

One Enchanted Afternoon

You've been told....
"Go for it."
"You only live once."
"Life is about taking risks."
"No regrets, man."

You see her across a campus lawn;
she is talking with a group of friends.
You drop your book bag and run towards her...
as your courage increases so does your velocity.

All conversation stops when you reach her.
Your heart is pounding, more from adrenaline than the run over.
Her startled look is replaced by one of curiosity,
making her all the more beautiful.

You grab her around the waist and draw her close
before you lose your nerve.
You kiss her full on the mouth.
If this were a movie, dramatic music would be playing,
and the camera shot would be slowly swirling around the two of you.

But this is not a movie....
She knees you in the groin...
before you hit the ground;
she punches you flush on the Adam's apple.

Rolling around on the grass, barking like a Harp seal,
you are struck about the ribs and head
with a barrage of swift and vicious kicks
from four or five pair of flip-flop covered feet.

When you come to...
your hands are cuffed behind you.
A campus cop is rinsing the pepper spray
from your swollen eyes with cool water
from a nearby hose.

Although burning, your eyes are able to focus
on your book bag, as it is picked up
and walked away.

•   •   •   •   •

Everyone laughed hard and long.

"Well, whaddya think fellas?" Matty asked beaming.

"Glad I never went to college," Ish said. "Them chicks is mean."

Daniel gave Matty a congratulatory slap on the back, knocking the wind out of him.

"Dude, that is funny as hell," Daniel said. "But for the record... none of us ever suggested you run up and plant one on a total stranger. We just said to go up and introduce yourself. Big difference."

"My imagination gets the best of me sometimes," Matty said once he was able to breathe again.

"Let it get the best of you," Ed said. "The imagery you create is outstanding... hilarious stuff."

"I like the unexpected twist that took," Leon said. "Right up our alley. Good writing, son."

"I agree wholeheartedly," Wayne added. "Bravo."

"I can't stop smiling," I said with all sincerity. "You guys never cease to amaze me. Daniel, show us what ya got... please."

"Sure. Now, let me warn you guys... first of all there is no humor involved, so don't expect any. Secondly, don't go reading too much into this one... it's just a poem... in two parts, by the way. Lastly, I decided this one worked better without a picture... in other words... I couldn't think of one that would work."

Scars

The Background:

I have scars
each one has a story.
I'm not proud of any of them... nor am I ashamed.
Scars that zigzag across the top of my knuckles;
something's gotta give
when flesh meets tooth and bone.
Scars like zippers around my shoulders from years
of wear and repair.
There is a scar on my hairline
I don't remember the details but I think
it involved a brick.
Numerous scars on my forearms from numerous sources.
There are buckshot scars on my ass.
If you are wondering, I was running away from trouble.
I was young... and stupid.
I have scars each one has a story

A Story

I knew a girl once in Pittsburgh
Bonnie was her name
Often, late at night after closing time
we would sit at a table, with very little conversation,
just enjoy the silence
the only audible sound
was the slow, rhythmic click of a ceiling fan.
We were not intimate, just friends,
the only time we had ever touched

was a brief, awkward hug after she heard that my dad had passed.
One night I noticed her staring at my hands.
She then hesitantly reached across the table
and began to gently trace one of my scars with her finger.
I had never been self-conscious about my scars...... until now.
I tensed under her touch, almost recoiled but I caught myself.
"Not very pretty, are they?"
She smiled, "Perfection is overrated... and boring."
At this I relaxed
"We all have scars." she continued, "Some are visible ... some are not."
I thought about that for a moment, and then I laughed,
"Funny, many of those scars are from my brothers... or my dad"
"Aren't most scars caused from ones we love?"
Lost in thought, I did not respond for the longest time.
Eventually, I looked up, but did not speak, just nodded.
The distance between us was closing,
and I was not sure if I was ready for that...
not ready for another scar...
another story.

•   •   •   •   •

There was a long, respectful silence. Ed then cleared his throat.

"Wow. That's another powerful poem."

"Your physical strength and presence are impressive, but not a match for your strength as a writer," Leon said.

"You can tell an interesting tale, big man," Matty said. "I agree; it's impressive."

"I was really moved by that," Wayne said.

"If it can move *Wayne,* then it..." Ish started to say.

We all shot Ish a look and he didn't finish his sentence. This was not the time for jokes or put-downs. I looked over at Wayne. He sat up taller and his eyes got bigger, but just for an instant... he took a deep breath then he relaxed.

"Great job, Daniel," I said quickly. "I really enjoyed that."

"I don't mean to pry or get personal," Ed said cautiously, leaning forward, "but is that story in any way connected to why you moved here?"

"I would have moved sooner or later for another reason... but... yeah... it helped get the wheels in motion."

"Do you regret that now?" Ed asked.

"Often," Daniel answered quietly, looking at his hands.

Once again, there was an awkward silence by the rest of the men as Daniel seemed to be deep in thought. He snapped out of it after a short time, and smiled.

"But, on the other hand, I'm glad I moved here and was lucky enough to meet such a great group of guys... and Ish, too."

"The feelin' is mutual, big man," Ish said beaming, not catching the dig.

"Well, for whatever reason you ended up here," I said, "I'm glad you did."

"Amen," Ish said.

"Ed - ready to present?"

"Anything for you, George."

Burying a Horse

The horse is dying and there is nothing I can do.
He is near thirty and has lived a good long life.
The backhoe is busted, the fix will be pricey and in the future.
I've never buried an animal this size with a shovel.
I had a cousin who claimed to have buried a cow this way.
He didn't say why, just laughed about it and shook his head.
I didn't question or doubt his claim; he's got more grit than I.

It's early in the day; the sun is low in the sky.
The ground is soft from recent rains.
If I'm going to do this, now is the time.

Cold muscles gradually limber up and loosen.
The digging is easy in the rich black earth and I settle into a steady rhythm.

EAST OF ANYWHERE

The rhythm is broken when the topsoil is replaced with rock and clay.
The shovel is moved to the side and I switch to a pickaxe to break up the soil.

Hours later, hands I thought tough, begin to blister.
Limbs, I thought strong, ache.

At dusk the vast hole is complete, the tools put back in the shed.
It's a long slow walk with the old gelding to the edge of the grave.
A chalk X is marked on his forehead where the bullet will enter.
I whisper my goodbye, and raise the gun to the mark.
There is a long hesitation.
I lower the gun.
Decide to put off 'til tomorrow something that needs to be done now.
I walk the horse back to his stall and head back to the house,
for a night of restless sleep.

•   •   •   •   •

The men all made positive remarks on the poem and how descriptive it was. Several commented on the picture and his use of shadow and light. Then Leon asked the question that was on all our minds.

"Wow, you had to do that?" Leon asked.

"Yeah, on Monday. I know your next question is; did I go through with it? I called the vet and had him do it by injection. It still wasn't easy; I had really grown fond of that ol' horse."

"I bet it never gets easy," Daniel said.

"When you work around animals, death is a part of it. They get sick, or injured, or just get old. You would not believe how many barn cats I've had and lost. I tell myself to not get attached to them... but I always do."

"I don't think I'd ever get used to that," Matty said.

"Honestly, I've reached the point where I have more reverence for life than I did when I was younger. I use to hunt, and I just don't have the heart for it anymore. I use to butcher my chickens but now I just collect their eggs and when they quit producing, I keep them as pets. Silly, I guess."

"Not silly at all," Daniel said. "Some men become harder and gruffer as they age; some don't change much at all. But others... perhaps the lucky ones... become gentler."

"Like you, Daniel?" Leon asked.

"Maybe."

"Ed, if you were still a policeman would this change have made you better at your job... or worse?" Matty asked.

"Interesting question. Better, I think. But, then again, I think my evolving didn't start to happen till long after I had retired."

"Well your life experiences, Ed and Daniel, have made for interesting material to write about," I said. "All of you for that matter... even our youngest poet. Okay, speaking of life experiences, ready to go Ish?"

"Hell yeah."

I Wish You Did Too

walking down the windy street
wearing nothing but these ripped jeans,
a threadbare black t-shirt,
and a pair of borrowed boots, two sizes too small.
the digital bank clock flashes the time, 11:24.
then the temperature, 35 degrees.
I'm not prepared for the weather.
don't know what I was thinkin,'
that's a problem...
I often don't think... or plan ahead.
not sure where I'm headed.
a warm building would be nice.
local library up ahead,
perfect.
thrust hands deep into pants pockets,
head down to avoid the wind.
pick up the pace, cut across the parking lot,
stop just before I bump into a young girl.

books in one hand car keys in the other.
she smiles but she is clearly not at ease...
not fear, more like... concern
"How are you?" she says
"I wish I had a coat."
"I wish you did too."

•   •   •   •   •

Once again the men were silent after the poem. Clearly impressed... and surprised.

"Who's a writer *now*, bitches?" Ish asked. "I could be the poet lariat!"

Not one person corrected him.

"You da *man*, Ish," Ed said. "That was good. True story?"

"Yep, told Daniel about it and, once again, he said it sounded like a poem. I came back an hour later with it written in a notebook and he helped me polish 'er up."

"Didn't need much," Daniel confirmed. "I just made a few suggestions. For example, he wanted to say, 'Wish I had me a coat'. I suggested he take out the 'me'.'"

"Did you fall in love with the girl, Ish?" Leon asked, grinning.

"Almost did, but I got to thinkin' that her concern for me was because she thought I was homeless."

"Where'd she get that idea?" Ed asked with a poker face.

"I don't rightly know, but it happens to me all the time. People will direct me to a shelter, and such. Here's a good one for ya; One time I was standing on the street corner holdin' a cupa' coffee, waiting for my cousin. Somebody walkin' past and put a five-dollar bill in my cup! Gave my coffee an awful taste. But, I bought me a Big Mac with the money... it was good too. My cousin wanted me to split it with him. I says, 'Jasper, hold out your *own* damn coffee cup'!"

"I like the artistry of the picture," Matty said. "I'm assuming by the look of the guy, it's not you."

"Too scrawny lookin'?" Ish asked.

"Too clean," Wayne clarified, softly.

"Well," I said quickly. "I think this is another example of how a simple life experience can be turned into a nice piece of art. Well done. Okay Wayne, what have you got for us?"

"More girlfriend issues I'm embarrassed to admit, but it felt good to write about it. *Extremely* therapeutic."

Covered with Kisses

You come home from work
To find a trail of small foil wrappers leading
To the bedroom
I am waiting for you there in bed
Covered with nothing but, (not roses petals, I remembered your allergy)
Kisses...
Hershey chocolate kisses.
After several hours of lying there, I nod off.
Unbeknownst to me you went out for drinks with coworkers.
A romantic, roaring fire in the fireplace combined with my body heat
Have melted the chocolate.
The dark stillness is broken by your blood-curdling scream.
I rise up looking like something from the La Brea Tar Pits.
Yes, I agree the stains are unsettling.
I'm sure the dry cleaner will understand.
Surely he's dealt with this before.

• • • • •

"Ho, Ho! Are you kidding me!? What kinda freakin' idiot would..."

That's all Ish got out. Without even looking over to him, Wayne backhanded Ish right across the forehead with a beefy right hand. Ish went toppling over backward and lay there, apparently knocked-out cold. Oddly, he still had a smirk on his face. Wayne stood up, smiled, nodded to the group and said, "See you next week, gentleman." Then he left, holding his right hand gingerly with the other, as if nothing had happened. The room was silent for a moment. Leon, Matty, and I sat there, in a state of shock. Ed was smiling and shaking his head. Daniel started chuckling, and then so did Ed.

"That shit did not just happen..." Matty said in wide-eyed astonishment.

Ish opened his eyes and slowly gave us a thumbs up. He continued to lie there with the same dumbass look on his face. No one rushed over to see if he was okay, myself included.

"Surreal," Leon mumbled with the same look as Matty.

"Didn't see that coming," I said. "I'm not sure my dad would have either. I should have talked to Ish sooner, and with more firmness, about his rude remarks to Wayne."

"I'm not sure it would have done any good," Daniel said calmly. "I've talked to him about it several times and he agreed with me. Yet he keeps on making dumbass comments."

"Not cool," Matty said, regaining his calm.

"I don't think it's in his DNA to be a jerk," Ed said. "Just poor upbringing and insecurity."

"Wow, I think Wayne got his point across," Leon said with a chuckle. "I guess that was the straw that broke the camel's back."

"That wasn't spontaneous," Daniel said. "That was calculated."

"I agree," Ed said.

"Enlighten me, gentlemen," I said.

"Yes, do tell," Leon added.

"Exhibit A," Daniel said. "Why would someone share or even *write* a poem that humiliating? He knew Ish would jump on it, giving him an excuse to blast him. I would wager that what Wayne wrote about never happened. I'm guessing that he needed something way over the top so Ish would have no choice but to take the bait... and it worked."

Matty, Leon, and I sat in amazement listening to Daniel as Ed shook his head in agreement.

"Fascinating...." Leon said, eyes wide again.

Ed jumped in. "Exhibit B," he said. "Wayne *never* sits next to Ish, but tonight he plants himself right next to him. He had a choice to sit to the right or left of Ish... as usual both sides were free. He needed to catch Ish off guard, and the best way to do that would be with a big right backhand that he wouldn't see coming, so he sat to the left of Ish."

"I saw him stretching and loosening up his shoulder in the hallway before he came in," Matty added excitedly. "I found it odd... thought it was an old marching band injury bothering him."

"Earlier this evening Ish made a crack, and Wayne's eyes got a little wide," Daniel said. "Wayne caught himself before he reacted. He needed Ish to say something that would justify the knockout. As soon as Ish said 'freakin' idiot', he unleashed on him."

"You have to admit," Ed said grinning. "It was a pretty clever setup."

"I've got to deal with this," I said with my face in my hands. "This is a poetry workshop not fight-club. If the university finds out about this, they might pull the plug on this project."

"Hemingway got into a fist fight with a poet once in Key West," Matty said.

"Wallace Stevens," Daniel clarified.

"Yeah, that's the dude!" Matty said.

"How cool would that be... to say you fought Ernest Hemingway?" Ed asked.

"Fellas!" I said raising my voice. "We have a guy, often mistaken for a homeless man, unconscious on the floor of a *university*... while we discuss fist fighting writers! Seriously?"

"Don't forget to add, 'in Key West'," Leon said.

"I'll take care of him," Daniel said reassuringly.

"Probably like another day at the office for you, Daniel," Ed said. "Need any help?"

"You could give us a lift. It might draw some unwanted attention if I were to carry him down the street or if I had him draped over my motorcycle. You could also open the door for me and check to make sure the hallway is clear. I'll take him to the ER to be checked, then to my place and keep an eye on him, make sure there is no brain damage."

"How would you be able to tell?" Leon asked.

"Good point... It looks like he's startin' to come around a little more... If he seems to have a severe concussion, they'll be able to tell at the ER. I'm pretty confident a skull x-ray would reveal nothing."

We all smiled at that last comment. Daniel threw Ish over his shoulder as if he were a dishrag and headed for the door right behind Ed. Ish lifted his head and looked over to us, he grinned a drunken, glassy-eyed grin and waved goodbye as they headed out the door.

WEEK SEVEN

Our session had ended so abruptly last week that I had forgotten to give them their assignment. I had to call them all that night in order to give them enough time to complete it. The guys had been getting along so well I thought it would be interesting to break into pairs and do a collaborative poem. The irony of this was lost on no one. They all got a chuckle out of it. I called Daniel first to see how Ish was doing. Daniel took all the precautions with Ish and said he was doing fine; thought he would be back to his old self... unfortunately... by the next day. He said that they had run into Wayne in the waiting room of the ER. Turns out that Wayne was getting his hand x-rayed. The two of them had a civil talk and even shook hands... gingerly. (I acted as if this was all new information, and that I had not been spying on them).

Daniel also offered to work with Ish on the collaboration poem. I was hoping that Ed would work with Ish. Daniel had already paid his dues by working with Ish on all the other poems. I agreed for several reasons, one being that logistically it might have been difficult for Ed and Ish to get together. In the end, the pairs were, Daniel and Ish, Ed and Wayne, and Leon and Matty.

The men came in and were rather subdued; they knew it was going to be awkward after the way class ended last week. Wayne arrived right before Ish, and sat down. He was quiet, but he always is. Ish came in. He did not sit; he walked right up to the circle of chairs and started talking.

"Hey, fellas," he began, his head hanging low. "I need to apologize for my behavior that led up ta last week's...uh... incident. Ya see... the gang of friends I growed up with, and still hangs out with, was always ripping on each other. Hell, even my own family was forever all over each other. It's a poor excuse, I know, but it's a bad habit I've developed that I aim ta correct. I've apologized ta Wayne. Daniel suggested... strongly suggested I might add, that I apologize to George and y'all as well. The big boy... er, Wayne, packs a powerful wallop. I deserved it."

"And I have apologized to Ish, as well," Wayne said. "It's not like me to resort to violence...it was wrong. I should have told him the comments were bothering me."

"We all are to blame as well," Ed said. "We should have said something. The rude comments were toxic to the chemistry of the group. And as friends, we should have stuck up for you."

"Agreed," Leon added.

"Daniel told me a couple of times to cool it with my insults and wise-ass comments," Ish said. "But I didn't listen."

"As the facilitator of this group I'm to blame for letting it go on," I said. "I don't tolerate hurtful comments in my classroom at school... I don't know why I let it go on here. I have been impressed by how well we have gotten along and how quick we all have become friends. I would hate to lose that. This group is special; it means the world to..."

"Okay, okay," Ish interrupted, "I didn't want this ta turn into a freakin' love fest. I said I was sorry and promise ta play nice. Let's move on."

"Kumbaya anyone?" Leon wisecracked.

Matty joined in on the wise-ass remark, "Great idea! George, can I run and get my guitar?"

"Alright, alright," I said, throwing my hands up in the air, embarrassed. "The point has been made."

"Now that we are all in a loving mood," Daniel said. "I think Ish and I should share first, because we wrote... wait for it... *love* poems."

"Have y'all noticed how sweet he is on me?" Ish asked.

"People are startin' to talk..." Leon said.

"You all thought Wayne had a wicked backhand," Daniel said straight-faced. "Would anyone like to experience mine?"

"Relax big man," Ish said. "I was just funnin' ya."

"Hang on," Ed said. "I did notice when you carried Ish out last week you treated him with such... tenderness."

"You're going to need that shovel again, Ed," Daniel said.

"Easy now," Ed said. "Just an observation."

Everyone chuckled... once they saw Daniel smiling.

"Are we done now?" Daniel asked. "Okay, not tryin' to show anybody up or anything, but we wrote *two* poems instead of just one, now these poems..."

"Ladies, gentleman... and Ish..." Leon barked. "I present to you the

World's *largest* teacher's pet..."

"Jealousy will get you nowhere, sir...and that's kind of ironic coming from a guy who wrote *three* poems one week... As I was saying, these poems are loosely based on a conversation we overheard at the bar one night. Of course, we embellished a *great* deal, solely for entertainment reasons. Then we decided to really challenge ourselves and put them to rhyme, causing us to embellish even more."

"Did ya mention we made up ninety-nine percent of the shit?" Ish asked.

"I did, partner, but I think they would've figured that out anyway. Here's the first one."

For You

I would paint the sky for you
tell a lie for you even
wear a suit and tie for you

I would hurt for you
shovel dirt for you
comb my hair and tuck in my shirt for you

I would take a loss for you
punch out your boss for you
brush my teeth and floss for you

I would sing the blues for you
hit the snooze for you
match my belt and shoes for you

I would buy flowers by the bunches for you
pack gluten-free lunches for you do
ten or more crunches for you

RICK THORPE

I would swim to France for you
learn to country line dance for you
even male enhance for you... (not that I need to)

I would spend my cash for you
heal this rash for you
get off the couch and take out the trash for you

I would be a clown for you
move across town for you
remember to put the toilet seat down for you

These things and more, I would do for you

• • • • •

"You've outdone yourselves," Leon said. "Stellar, absolutely stellar."

"I agree," Matty added. "Brilliant."

"I think you have the makings of a country song," I said.

"I thought me the same dang thing, George!" Ish said excitedly. "We created a pretty romantic fella, did we not?"

"Some would say that," Leon said, "not many, but some... Your circle of friends, for sure."

"You guys never cease to amaze me," Ed said grinning. "I mean this with the deepest respect... I would have never guessed when we all first met that you two would be writing stuff like that. Never judge a book by its cover."

"Amen," Wayne said.

"I can't wait to see the next one," I said.

"Well, here you go," Daniel said with a hint of pride.

And I for You

I will moisturize these lips for you
buy salt and vinegar chips for you
throw away my chains and whips for you

I will look at no other for you
evict your deadbeat brother for you
attempt electrolysis on Mother for you

I will dive in and take the plunge for you
look at past transgressions and expunge for you
lift, run, squat, and lunge for you

I will be there and see it through for you
return books that are overdue for you
remove this misspelled tattoo for you

I will sing Gregorian chants for you
try to wear skinny pants for you
upgrade my implants for you

I'll write poems or a paperback for you
stifle this smoker's hack for you
shave my legs and back for you

I will develop a symbiosis for you
tolerate morning halitosis for you
straighten my scoliosis for you

I will live in a hut for you
suck in my beer gut for you
exfoliate my butt for you

All these things I will do for you, my love

• • • • •

"I thought, there's no way in hell you guys would be able to top that first one," Leon said, "but you just might have. This character, be it woman or man, has a higher vocabulary than the first one."

"Like parents, we're proud of both our babies," Daniel said.

"I don't believe Williams, Whitman, or Frost ever used the words electrolysis, expunge, and halitosis in the same poem," I said thoughtfully.

"Hell, I've never heard of half them words," Ish said, "but it's still funny to me."

"I might be mistaken, but I think I'm dating the person you wrote about," Wayne said.

"It would be interesting to see a picture of these two love birds," Matty said.

"You have interesting characters hanging out in that bar... I need to get out more," Ed said.

"Okay, Ed, can you and Wayne present next?" I asked.

"Sure, and I thought following Leon was difficult... Our poem is based on a story Wayne's father told him. We hope you like it."

Blind Date 1975

I park my Ford Pinto and walk briskly
up to the front door.
Yet... I hesitate outside the bar.
It's been awhile.
I'm sure I can do this,
I just need... I just need...
What do I need?
Nothing.
I'm fine just the way I am.
Thick around the middle, sure.
Hair thinning, yep.

Oh well, here goes.
I take off my glasses
and shove them in the jacket pocket of my leisure suit.
Wow, it's dark in here... thank God.
The Bee Gees '*Jive Talking*' is blaring on the stereo.

RICK THORPE

I hope this girl is not hard of hearing.
There she is.
Well, I assume it's her,
blonde hair, red dress.
Wow, from here she appears to be built like
Sargent Pepper Anderson from the TV show *Police Woman*!

I throw my shoulders back and stroll over.
She brings a cigarette up to her lips.
I dig my lighter out of my pocket.
In one smooth gesture I bring a flame up to her cigarette.

A coy smile appears on her lips.
In a throaty whisper she says,
"I think you would look good in your glasses."
"Uh, thank you. How did you know I wore glasses?"
"You just lit my French fry."
I laugh nervously,
as the smell of
burnt potatoes
fills the air.

• • • • •

"Good job fellas," Daniel said enthusiastically. "That ending took me by surprise."

"Yes, and I like all the '70's references throughout," Leon added. "I even got some of them!"

"I'm curious about the collaboration process," I said. "Daniel and Ish have worked together before, but this was new for you guys. How did it work for you two?"

Wayne nodded to Ed. Ed spoke first.

"Like on any project someone needs to take the lead. Wayne took the lead because he had an idea in mind and I did not. I helped by making a few suggestions along the way. Since I was alive during 1975, I was able to help in that respect."

"He's being too humble," Wayne said. "He was a great collaborator. His suggestions were made tactfully and they were right on target."

"Ed was nice 'cause he feared gettin' bitch-slapped," Ish said while rubbing his forehead.

"It did enter my mind."

"I wondered why you sat so far away," Wayne said with a mock frown.

"Seriously, we got along great and we're pleased with what we came up with. I found Wayne to be intelligent and creative. Isn't that picture great? Totally his idea."

Ish got a sly grin on his face as a brown stream of tobacco juice dribbled down his chin. This aroused my curiosity, and then concerned me, as he did not have a receptacle of any sort to spit in.

"Go fetch your guitar, Matty. I feels another love fest comin' on."

"Easy Ish," Daniel said. "I'm not draggin' your ass to the ER two weeks in a row."

"Thank you for showing true constraint, Wayne," I said. "Leon and Matty, you're up."

"Okay, let me set this up," Leon said. "I had this idea for a poem based on a quiz I plan on giving to my students that I will know will go poorly. I came up with the questions and Matty, thinking as a high school kid would, came up with the answers. And as you will see, he absolutely hits it out of the park."

Your Last History Quiz

As I *hope* you recall, we took the final quiz of the year, yesterday. I graded the quiz last night and found it quite enlightening. Needless to say, you all did as I expected, quite poorly. Below is the quiz again. For each question I have supplied what I think are the top three most ridiculous answers, supplied by you, the members of this class. Enjoy, and good riddance.

This will be your final quiz of the year. Two points for every correct answer, one point for every attempt at an answer. Listed below are ten partial quotes from famous Americans. These quotes have been on posters posted around this classroom all year until today. Finish the quote the best you can.

1. Franklin Roosevelt- "The only thing we have to fear.................................."
    A. cafeteria food
    B. the scary dude with no nose in the Harry Potter Movies
    C. failing this test

2. Thomas Jefferson- "The cement of this union is.........................."
    A. crumbling
    B. available in bags at Home Depot
    C. still wet, please do not write your initials in it

3. Nathan Hale- "I regret that I have but one life.."
    A. two lives would be awesome, but kind of schizophrenic
    B. if I was Hindu, I could come back and try it again
    C. cats sure are lucky

4. Franklin Roosevelt- "December 7th, 1941 is a day that........................."
    A. was very important for numerous reasons
    B. many stores start their Christmas sale C. the old ass teacher that created this test, started his career on

5. Theodore Roosevelt- "Speak softly.."
    A. in the library
    B. my parents are in the next room
    C. I have a hangover

6. Abraham Lincoln- "A house divided is.."
    A. very drafty
    B. a realtor's worst nightmare
    C. probably a split level

7. Harry Truman- "America was not built on fear, America was built on........."
    A. credit
    B. the coast and worked its way backward
    C. property that belonged to the Indians

8. Ronald Reagan- "Mr. Gorbachev, tear down.."
   A. that privacy fence
   B. the set, the play is over
   C. that hideous wallpaper in the Kremlin, it clashes with the curtains

9. Patrick Henry- "I know not what course others will take, but as for me, give me.................."
   A. diesel mechanics
   B. a course with more chicks and less dudes
   C. a chance to retake this one

10. Admiral Perry- "I have met the enemy and they......................................."
    A. share my bedroom
    B. are in the teacher's lounge
    C. be ugly

197

•   •   •   •   •

"You're right, Leon," Daniel said, "Matty's answers are dead on funny. But give yourself credit; you set him up with some great quotes."

"You lobbed him some softballs, and he crushed them," Ed added. "And the look on those three kids faces is priceless."

"Yeah, I told them to look like clueless dumbasses. In actuality, those are three of the brightest kids I know."

"Getting back to the partnership. That was another successful pairing," Wayne said. "You gentlemen complement each other well. Nice grouping, George."

"Thanks," I said, "but you guys deserve the credit. This had potential to be a bust. I would like to think it would have worked with other pairings just as well."

"I was not sure how this collaboration thing was going to work," Matty said. "But I really enjoyed it." Then he added with a sad smile, "Leon reminds me of my dad."

"And he, my son," Leon said, matching the sad smile with his own.

"This partner thing," Ish said, "It didn't suck."

"I'll take that as a compliment," Daniel said dryly.

"I'm just messin' with ya big man. You's worked with me on my stuff since day one, and I'm grateful. It was nice to be able to help you for a change. I was proud of what we came up with."

"We're cool," Daniel said. "You're growin' on me, dude... which scares me."

"Collaboration does not always go so smoothly," I said. "It's not easy to give up an idea, a concept, something you believe in. Compromise can be tough, you have to be able to give and take and have thick skin."

"Okay, Brother George, what challenge have you got for us this week?" Leon asked.

"This is going to be a real test of how creative you can be."

Leon started rubbing his hands together in eager anticipation.

"Bring it."

"In my classroom I have a set of magnetic poetry," I said. "It's a bunch of words in a box and the goal is to pull out a bunch of the words and make a poem, using some of them. It's possible to use all the words you pull out, but they end up sounding like some weird, surreal dream. Usually these are very funny. Many people use these poem magnets on their refrigerators. I use them -"

"I bet ol' William Carlos Williams would have loved a set of those babies!" Ish interrupted with a shout.

"Bet you're right," I said, annoyed at the interruption, but pleased at the connection he had made.

"Woulda' driven his wife bonkers," Leon added with a laugh.

"As I was saying... I use them on a chalkboard or on the tops of desks. Another challenge is to create a poem *title* when you are given a handful of random words, and then write a poem based on that. So that is what I have decided to do with you. I will give you three words, a noun or pronoun, a preposition, and a verb. I've already separated them out and put them into these three bags. With these three words, and any others you want to add, create the title of a poem."

"You're right," Ed said with a look of concern, "that is a challenge."

"Okay, I'll randomly pull out six nouns."

I pulled out six words and laid them out in front of me.

"They are the nouns: *pocket, glass, road, cafe', ocean*, and the pronoun, *you*. I'm going to toss you each a word."

Without looking at which word I was grabbing, I tossed each man a word. Most of them smiled and nodded.

"Good, next I'll do the same with verbs."

I repeated the same process.

"They are: *getting, lying, looking, meeting, having*, and *putting*."

I threw one verb to each man. You could see the wheels turning as they thought about how to make the two words they had fit. While they looked at the words, I pulled out the prepositions.

"Alright, here are your prepositions: *out, at, through, in, on*, and *by*."

"Can we tweak them a little bit if we need to? Matty asked. "Like add or remove a prefix or suffix, or make it plural?"

"Sure, sure... as long as you use a form of the word. We have time right now to work on your titles. Move the words around, try different combinations, and see what you come up with. Please don't stress over it, this is just an exercise and it's just for fun."

The men studied their words; some of them were talking to themselves, to hear what it sounded like. Only Ish was at ease and he was the one I worried about the most. He had his hands folded behind his head with a big, tobacco-stained, smirky grin on his face.

"Got me a title already, bitches," Ish said. "The rest of y'all must be a buncha slow learners... passengers on the short bus!"

"A title is the easy part," Wayne said slowly, as if talking to a child, "Writing a poem to go under it is the true test."

"Gots a plan for that too," Ish said with a coy grin.

The rest of the session, the men worked on their titles, and then started brainstorming for the poem itself. I thought this was going to be a good idea; now I'm having my doubts. I guess we will find out.

WEEK EIGHT

By the look on the men's faces, my fears were not justified. Everyone walked in with a smile on his face... even Wayne. It's amazing that we have met for eight weeks now and I have not had one man be absent. Something must be going right.

"Well, Gents, I know this assignment was somewhat unorthodox, but if I know you like I think I know you, you all were able to come up with something clever and entertaining. I drew names before class started, so Daniel, you are up first... if that's okay with you."

"Sure. Let me give you the background story first. The noun that I was given was *café*, being an art guy, my first thought was Van Gogh's painting, *'The Night Café'*. My verb was *'meeting'*, and the preposition was *at*, so *'meeting at a café'* was a given, but meeting who? So I thought, 'What would Leon do?' Then it came to me, that I should meet Van Gogh. I asked Leon for some advice, and he had some great suggestions."

"It was an honor," Leon said while bowing at the waist. "His clever idea inspired my poem, as you will see."

"Great, let's see it, Daniel," I said.

Meeting at The Night Café

I met Vincent at The Night Café.
Theo, his brother, had set up the meeting.
Theo said to look for the table with the vase of sunflowers.
This was not really necessary;
I knew what he looked like from the self-portraits of his I had viewed.
I would recognize him with or without a beard, hat or left ear.
He was there waiting for me just as I had imagined,
shock of red hair with a beard to match.
"I'm so glad to finally meet you. I've admired your work for a long time."
He turned his head slightly to his left.
He was self-conscience about his disfigured left ear,
but I mistook the gesture as a sign that he was hard of hearing,
so I spoke louder.
Other patrons at the café stopped their conversations and looked our way.
I spied Paul Gauguin sitting a few tables over.
He was with two beautiful, colorfully dressed Tahitian women.
I started to speak to him but before the words left my mouth,

he silenced me by bringing an index finger to his lips, shaking his head no.
I thought he wanted me to be quiet,
but then I realized he did not want me to alert Vincent of his presence.
He turned his back to us and picked up a mango.
To Vincent I said, "Damn, if you don't look just like Kirk Douglas."
"I get that a lot," he said proudly, "I loved him in *From Here to Eternity*."
I nodded and agreed.
I didn't have the heart to tell him that it wasn't Douglas in that famous film,
but Burt Lancaster.
Our meals arrived.
Vincent noticed that both of our meals included potatoes,
mine with fries, his with a side of hash browns.
"Well," he commented, "it looks like *we're* the 'Potato Eaters'."
I laughed at the reference to his famous painting.
This pleased him that I got the joke.
His paintings are always so intense; it threw me that he had a sense of humor.
We made small talk while we ate.
I ask what inspired him to paint so many haystacks.
He shrugged, "They were close by and the art store had a great deal on yellow and brown paint."
I nodded and then he added,
"Did you know in each haystack I painted a tiny little needle?"
"Really?"
"No, I'm just messing with ya."
I laughed and slapped the table almost spilling his absinthe.
I then asked if he liked the song Don McLean wrote about him.
"Well, naturally I was flattered. I'm impressed with the poetry of the song, but it's really a downer, don't you think?
He smiled, and added, "And it's harder than heck to dance to."
I agreed, "Definitely not a toe tapper."
He then noticed Gauguin sitting behind us, "Hey Paul, lend me an ear!"
Gauguin ignored him.
Vincent pointed to his mutilated left ear, "This is entirely his fault you know."
"A spat that got out of hand?"
"Yep, and he hasn't spoken to me since. Professional jealousy if you ask me."

He looked back over at the two Tahitian woman and shouted,
"Don't trust him ladies! He'll wine you and dine you and the next thing you
know you'll be posing with half your clothes off!"
They blushed and laughed nervously.
I, too, felt uncomfortable and quickly changed the subject.
"Vincent, there is one question I've been dying to ask you."
"Ask away."
"Why do you use so much freaking paint? It must have been a real bitch to
clean those brushes."
He appeared to be thinking, then distracted by movement.
Two large men in white coats had stepped up to our table.
Embroidered on the chest of their coats are the words 'Saint-Paul Asylum'.
"It appears our time is up my friend," he stated with a hint of sadness.
"I'm sorry you have to go," I replied with great sadness.
"Oh, they're not here for me."
The two men walked past Vincent and lifted me up out of my seat by my arms.
"Wait, I have a flight to Paris at nine o'clock! I'm meeting Toulouse-Lautrec
at the Moulin Rouge!"
"Don't be late!" Vincent shouted, as I was being dragged out of the café.
"Henri will get *short* with you if he thinks you've stood him up!"
The last thing I saw as I was being pulled out the door
was Gauguin's smirking face,
mango juice running down his chin.

•   •   •   •   •

"That ranks up there with your other great poems," I said. "Cerebral and clever. Well done."

"I did *not* see that twist coming at the end!" Matty said. "Fantastic."

"I agree," Ed said. "You put some work into that one, and it paid off."

Daniel seemed proud of the praise and just a little embarrassed at the attention. He looked down at his hands, as he often does, but a slight grin stayed on his face for quite a while.

"It's like a dream," Wayne said.

"Or a trip," Ish mumbled. Then realized he said it louder than he had wanted to. "Ya know... like a nice vacation."

"Good save," I said. "Okay, Wayne you are up next."

"Mine does not need much explaining. My three words were, *ocean*, *having*, and *by*. I will add... it's brief... but I'm proud of it."

Having Breakfast by the Ocean

Sitting on the edge of the pier
Enjoying a late breakfast
The sun just peaking
over the mangroves
A slight breeze ruffles my napkin
Above me a seagull glides past
Hoping for a handout
I look down into water
smooth as glass
Looking back at me
is a Manatee
He is eating a Belgian waffle
loaded with whipped cream
I realize it is just my reflection
Tomorrow I will start my day
with fruit and perhaps
a low-fat yogurt

• • • • •

"Now that *one* is funny as hell!" Ish shouted. "I gets that one."

"You have a great sense of humor, Wayne." Ed said. "Like Daniel's poem, I did not see that ending coming."

"Thanks, I thought you guys would like it... especially Ish. I saw my reflection recently, and I thought it was someone else. I can't believe how *large* I've gotten. I need to do something about it. I don't like people making fun of my size, but a little self-deprecating humor, occasionally, is good for the soul."

"The brevity of it makes it work as well," Leon said. "You do a great job of being concise, and yet very witty."

"Where did you get the picture?" Matty asked.

"It was on my computer from a vacation I took to Florida a few years ago. I thought it would work with this poem."

"Great job, Wayne," I said. "Okay Matty, let's see what ya got."

"Those are hard acts to follow, but I, as well, like what I wrote. Just to give you a little background; the three words I received were, *road*, *lying*, and *on*. The poem is loosely based on a football coach I had in high school. He often would start practice with a story or a life lesson. Unfortunately, many of my teammates didn't understand his parables. He took it in stride though; he had a great sense of humor. Well, here goes."

Walnuts Lying on the Road

"Circle up boys... helmets off... take a knee."

"Which knee, Coach?"

"Either one, Gary... right or left, pick your favorite..."

"Before we start practice today, I want to tell you a story..."

"Is it the story about how you *almost* got a scholarship to Notre Dame?"

"No, this is a new story."

"Good, we've heard that other one *a lot*."

"Thanks, David. I'll make a note of that...

Every morning I take the same route to school.

About two miles before I get here I pass a large walnut tree.

Now this tree is very close to the road.

In the Fall, this time of year, the walnuts from the tree begin to drop.

I've also noticed a high number of dead squirrels."

"Is it due to high cholesterol, Coach? My uncle was found dead on the road, Mom said he had high cholesterol."

"I don't think so, Ted. Most squirrels try to stick to a low-fat diet."

"Is it gang related?"

"That's not likely, but I guess anything is possible.

Come to think of it... there was some graffiti on the tree."

"Domestic violence?"

"No, only during mating season."

"A drunk driver?"

"Probably not... Coach Brink retired last year."

"I bet it was the cops!"

"An internal investigation found the cops innocent...
remember... furry lives matter. Now *please* let me finish this story.
It *appears* they are being hit by cars while trying to retrieve the walnuts."

"Why would cars be retrieving walnuts, Coach?"

"The squirrels, Doug, the squirrels were getting the walnuts."

"Oh! That makes more sense."

"Continuing on with my story, I thought this odd,
because most of the walnuts were in the *grass* not on the road.
Why take a risk on getting a walnut on the road when you could get one
safely in the grass?"

"Maybe the squirrels on that road are dumb, Coach."

"That crossed my mind... but then it hit me...
they were just trying to get out of work."

"Coach?"

"Yes, Vince."

"Do squirrels have jobs?"

"No, squirrels don't have jobs, but it takes a lot of *work* to get to the inside
of a walnut hull, and walnuts on the *road* are already opened up from cars
and trucks running over them."

"Coach, I'm confused, it sounds like they are dumb *and* smart."

"Well, I don't think it's a matter of intelligence.
I think the temptation is too great when they see the work is already done
for them. In life when you take a shortcut and don't do the work yourself,
there is often a price to pay."

"So what you are saying, Coach, is, 'Don't leave your nuts on the road'."

"Well... that is good advice, but..."

"I know, I know, Coach! 'Grassy nuts are better than asphalt nuts'."

"Thanks Kirk, but..."

"That's not the point, you dorks! Coach's message is, 'Don't let someone
else smash your nuts, smash them yourself'."

"All of you are just a little off base, but hey, at least you were listening...
for a change...
Okay, we've talked enough, we need to start practice, strap 'em up."
"I think it's too dark to practice, Coach."
"Your helmet is on backwards again, Gary."
"Sorry, Coach."
"It's okay, son... hustle up and join your teammates."

'Lord, it's going to be a long season...'

•   •   •   •   •

"Knocked it right through the uprights!" Ed said.

"Not only was it humorous," Leon said, "you captured the goofy nuance of high school kids, but the patience of a veteran teacher and coach. Good job, kid... But you're walking on thin ice with the 'furry live matter', line."

"I'm sorry. Did I offend you?"

"Nah, it's cool. Some people might not like it, but I think it's funny."

"Played ball did ya?" Ish asked. "No offense, but ya look kinda' skinny for a baller."

"Not all of us were blessed with your... *athletic* physique, Ish," Wayne said, rolling his eyes.

"That's true... Again... I didn't mean to offend, and I'm sorry if I did. He just don't strike me as a football type."

"I know it's hard to believe," Matty said, "but I played football. I was a receiver. I got to play a little bit, I enjoyed it... Did you play ball, Ish?"

"A buncha dudes a grabbin' each other, wrestlin' each other to the ground. Then prancin' off to take a hot shower together? Lemme tell ya somethin', that don't work for this guy."

"It's not for everyone," Matty said. "I bet Daniel played. Am I right?"

"Yep," Daniel said with a nod, and offered no more.

"Drafted in the second round," Ed chimed in.

"You're lucky to be alive, Daniel." Ish said. "Had an uncle that was drafted... went to 'Nam... never came back."

"Not the military draft, Ish, the NFL draft," Ed corrected.

"Once a cop, always a cop," Daniel murmured, eyes down.

"I'm sorry, buddy, I knew your name sounded familiar, so I did a little research. I know you're a private person. I didn't mean to reveal anything you didn't want revealed."

"It's okay; I wasn't hiding it. It just never came up... till now."

"Is that true, Daniel?" Leon asked excitedly. "Second round? What happened... if you don't mind me asking?"

Daniel took a deep breath and exhaled slowly.

"I was talked into playing football in high school by a guidance counselor as an outlet for some minor anger issues I was dealing with. I was pretty good at it and was able to get a scholarship, which was cool because there is no way I would have been able to afford college. I played well in college, obviously, and the word was out I was going to be picked in one of the upper rounds.

"I had mixed feelings. It was an honor to be one of the better ball players in the country but at the same time, I was really getting tired of the grind of football. I had other things I wanted to pursue."

"What team drafted you?" Leon asked.

"The Lions. I went to training camp and held my own. But it was very cut-throat and I wasn't sure if my heart was in it anymore. Then a very personal family matter came up, and I basically told them, 'Thanks, but no thanks and left the team. Detroit was an interesting city, so I stayed for a while doing odd jobs. The rest is history."

"That's a pretty cool story," Matty said. "Looks like you made the right decision with all the stuff out there about brain damage and the complications from multiple concussions."

"I think about that when I start to second guess my decision. Football was good to me, and I have many positive memories. I'm okay with how it all played out... Okay, who's up next?"

"Ed, you're up," I said.

"Okay. My three words were: *pocket, in, and putting,* which I shortened to *put.* Here you go."

When I Die put an Acorn in My Pocket

When I die
bury me in a cheap pine box.
Bury me in the pasture
on the hill
near the barn.
Bury me shallow.
Make the horses run
by my grave,
smack them on the rump
if you have to.
I want their thundering
hooves to rattle my bones.

When I die
bury me in that old
green flannel shirt.
You know the one,
faded and worn thin,
splattered with gray paint.

When I die
bury me with an acorn
in my right breast pocket.
Let the oak
that will one day
burst forth
from that black fertile soil
grow tall and straight.
Let it shade
those horses
as they graze
at my feet.

• • • • •

"Very nice!" Leon said. "It's simple, creates a great visual with or without the pictures."

"Cool poem," Matty said. "It definitely has a cowboy or Western feel to it."

"I agree," Daniel added. "And it fits your personality. Great job, Ed."

"Thanks, fellas. I was kinda shooting for a cowboy vibe."

"Cowboy poetry is actually pretty popular," I said. "There is even a Cowboy Poetry Society. I think Ed would fit right in."

"When I was a kid I remember watching a cowboy poet on *The Tonight Show*," Leon said. "My dad loved that guy. I believe he was a vet."

"Yeah, that was Dr. Baxter Black," I said. "I believe he is still very active in the writing world."

"I enjoy him on the radio, clever guy," Daniel said.

"Hey, Ed, are ya gonna be buried like a cowboy, with them boots on?" Ish asked.

"Probably not."

"What are ya, 'bout a size thirteen?" Ish asked, looking down at Ed's well-worn work boots.

"Yep, thirteen. How about I leave you my boots in my will?"

"Well, that would be just grand. Thirteen is a little big, but I'll make 'em work. Thanks my friend."

"No problem. They've got steel toes, protect your feet if you drop a pizza box or pool stick."

"As fit as Ed is," Daniel said, "and comparing both of your lifestyles, he might outlive you, Ish."

"Yeah, most of the men in my family don't make it past forty. It's been concernin' me, I was thinkin' 'bout takin' up joggin' ta increase my odds."

"Did you have a friend who left you some running shoes in his will?" Leon asked.

"I wish! No, I picked me up a pair at a yard sale. Pretty good shape too, 'cept for a crack in the bottom of one of 'em, which I did not know 'bout 'till I stepped in a puddle. I slapped some duct tape on it and she's good as new."

"If you're concerned for your health," Wayne advised, "you might want to give up the chewing tobacco as well."

"That habit is gonna be hard ta break," Ish said with a yellow stained grin.

"Been dippin' a long time?" Daniel asked.

"Started when I was 'bout eight."

"I believe it's illegal to sell tobacco, in any form, to a minor," Wayne said.

"Didn't buy it as a kid... stole it, a pinch here a pinch there, from my pap."

"He ever catch you doin' that?" Leon asked.

"Oh yeah, he whupped my ass good... had to start stealin' from Ma."

"Sounds like your family was as colorful as mine," Daniel said with a laugh.

"No, we was all white."

"Moving on," I said. "Leon, you are next."

"Cool... Like I said I was inspired by Daniel's use of a conversation with someone famous from a different time period. He graciously gave me the greenlight. My words were, *glass, looking,* and *through*. The title I created was a no-brainer, 'Through a Looking Glass'. I was thinking of doing a poem about Lewis Carroll or Alice in Wonderland, but I couldn't come up with a darn thing. Daniel mentioned that a looking glass can be a mirror, a magnifying glass, or a telescope. That's when I decided to do a poem about Galileo. Here you go..."

Through a Looking Glass

"Galileo Galilei come down here pronto!"

"What is it now, Mama?"

"What are you looking at with that spyglass?"

"I don't call it a spyglass Mama; I call it a perspicillum."

"A silly name for a silly contraption, now answer! What are you looking at!"

"I'm looking at the stars and... other things..."

"Where did you get it anyway?"

"I ordered it from two spectacle makers from the Netherlands."

"You are the one making a *spectacle*... out of yourself!"

"Madre, you don't get it. Here, look through the glass at the Torre Pendente."

"It looks very tiny, how is this helpful to anyone?"

"You are looking through the wrong end, try it this way."

"Oh my! Sure, it is much bigger, but it is very crooked smart guy!"

"Mama, everyone knows the Tower of Pisa is leaning!"

"Never mind smart guy! I got a call from Sophia Gamba."

"A call? The telephone is hundreds of years away."

"Okay, okay, a visit. Happy now?"

"And..."

"She say you are using this device to see in her daughter's bedroom window!"

"This is not true! I am looking at heavenly bodies!"

"Does one of those heavenly bodies belong to Marina Gamba?"

"No Mama, I'm not spying on Marina. Perhaps she should close her curtains!"

"Why can't you play the lute like your father and brother?"

"Chicks don't dig the lute Mama, it's boring."

"So what do they like, Science, Math? Physics perhaps?"

They like fame."

"What?"

"Fame. Everyone is attracted to fame. And one day I will be famous."

"You?"

"Yes, so famous they will name moons after me, mention me in rock songs!"

"The world doesn't revolve around you, Galileo."

"I know; it revolves around the Sun."

"Hush, my figlio! Do you want the Church to hear you?"

"But Copernicus stated that -"

"Copernicus! Copernicus! Copernicus! I'm sick of hearing about Copernicus!"

"But he is brilliant..."

"Enough! You are grounded to this house young man!"

"House arrest?"

"Get used to it. Go to your room and leave the spyglass here."

"So unfair! I wonder if Newton's mother will treat him this way?"

•   •   •   •   •

"Another good one, Leon," Matty said. "Did it take some research?"

"Yep. I knew some things about him. The research was as interesting as the writing was fun."

"We've used the word *clever* quite a bit," Ed said."But it applies with this poem as well. You need to read it more than once to catch some of the inside humor."

"Another enjoyable poem, Leon." Wayne said. "The photograph is very unique. How did you get the effect of looking through an old-time telescope?"

"I took apart an old pair of binoculars and held the lens and the casing that holds it, in front of my camera. I kept messing with it to get just the right amount of distortion."

"Who's the gal?" Ish asked. "She looks..."

"That's my daughter," Leon said, cutting him off, then, pointing a finger at Ish. "Be very careful how you finish that sentence."

"She looks... she looks... very smart."

"You're learnin'," Daniel said.

"But she ain't near as dark as you," Ish said.

"He takes his foot out of his mouth only to put it right back in," Daniel said.

"I may be Dominican but her mother was German," Leon said calmly.

"Good work, Leon," I said. "Ish, you're the last one tonight."

"All right. Here ya go; I hope y'all like it."

You... Get Out!

You know what two words I've probably heard the most in my life?

Does it start with F and end with off?

No... but come to think of it... that would be a close second.

I'm not really that curious, but I'm bored, so go ahead, enlighten me.

Long as I can remember, I've heard the words, 'Get out!' quite a bit.

No kidding?

At ten, I says 'Hey teacher ya gots chalk dust on your boobs.' She points to the door, says, 'Get out!'

Ruining your chances to be teacher's pet.

In high school I went to my girlfriend's house to meet her parents.

First impressions are very important.

I says to my girl, 'Man oh man, your mom is hotter than you are!' She gets mad and says, 'Get out!'

Probably should have kept that to yourself.

I told a bus driver he should get a toupee that matched the color of the hair growin' out his ears.

Let me guess... he said, 'Get out!'

Yep... Another time, me and my cousin went to this new strip club to... you know... check it out.

It's good to support local businesses...

So this real big ol' gal comes out, and I says to my cousin, 'Damn, I hope that pole don't snap.'

Let me guess, you said it a little too loud?

The music had cut out right as I was shoutin' it. Man, she was madder than a hornet!

Bet she said more than just, 'Get out.'

Yep... She cursed me out somethin' awful, words I never heard of. Bouncer said, 'Get out!', too.

Fella's just doin' his job.

Went to a Denny's once, and the manager said, 'Get out!', soon as I walked in.

The sign reads, 'No shirt, No shoes, No service'. Which were you missing?

I was wearin' both shirt and shoes... sign didn't say nothin' 'bout pants.

Seriously? Dude, are you that clueless?

My cousin thought it was funny... 'parently the manager did not.

Some people have a warped sense of humor.

I hear ya.

Well look, it's closin' time... You need to settle up... That'll be fourteen dollars.

Seems I'm a little short this week... can I hit ya up on payday?

Get out.

•   •   •   •   •

"Autobiographical I assume?" Leon asked.

"I don't know about that, but all that shit really happened ta me!"

"Who would have guessed that?" Leon said. "I really like it."

"Thank ya."

"Good work, Ish," Ed said. "Did Daniel help you edit the poem or is he the other voice in it?"

"Both."

"I'm a muse," Daniel said.

"Thanks buddy, I was amused myself. It was fun to write."

"Your interesting life has made for good material to write about," Matty said.

"And my folks thought I was a screw-up."

"You showed them," Wayne said.

"Good work Ish," I said. "Good job everyone. That was another productive week for the group. Next session is our last time to meet. I've skirted around talking about the reason why we are here, the fact that all of you are suffering some kind of loss. I've put-off bringing it up for two reasons. The first reason is I wanted you all to be comfortable with each other before we talked about something that was deeply personal. The second reason I waited so long was that, as you all know, my dad was the expert in this sort of thing not me. I'm still not really sure the path we've taken is the same path he would have taken -"

"Sorry to interrupt, George," Ed said, "but I think the role of the facilitator is to steer the group in the right direction. You've done that. I think your dad would be pleased and proud."

"Thanks. I appreciate that. Next week I would like to open up the floor for us to share why you are here, the source of your grief... but only if you are comfortable doing so. You have time to think about it. Your final poem can be about your loss or about closure... but again, if you are not ready for that just write whatever you feel like writing. I don't want our last time together to be a downer, but the healing process, like your photos, are a mixture of dark and light."

"Chiaroscuro," Matty said quietly.

The men were silent. They all seemed to be thinking their own private thoughts. Ed broke the silence.

"Several weeks ago we talked about coming out to my place. Would anyone object to having our last session there?"

"I'm okay with that," I said. "It would be nice to have our last meeting in a peaceful setting."

"Great idea, I'm in," Daniel said.

"Ditto," Ish said.

"I'll need a ride," Matty said. "I doubt if the bus line runs by Ed's place."

Leon leaned over and mussed up Matty's already unruly hair. "Got ya covered, kid... like that pencil that covered you in that drawing."

"The pollen count is finally down," Wayne said with a sigh of relief. "I'm in as well."

"I'll put my address and my phone number on the chalkboard," Ed said. "Come an hour early and I'll feed y'all. Please don't ask if you can bring anything... I'll cover everything."

"Can we butcher a hog?" Ish asked excitedly.

"Sorry buddy, I don't raise pigs. I was thinking of something simple on the grill."

"Cool, it's settled," I said. "Thanks, Ed. If everyone could bring seven copies of your poem or email it to me and I'll make the copies for you. See everyone next week at Ed's place."

The class went well; the men came through again. Only one more session. It's gone fast. I hope Ed was right about my role as a facilitator. I like these men and I don't want to cheat them.

WEEK NINE

I arrived early to give Ed any help he might need and to set up the camera. I was sad about this being our final session together. I never would have guessed that I would have grown to like these men so much. They were clever, interesting, and humorous.

Ed and I sat on the front porch waiting for the others to arrive. His easy manner made it seem like you were talking to an old friend. His farm and house were a reflection of the man himself, peaceful.

All the men arrived at about the same time. As Daniel was parking his motorcycle, Ish waved him over. Ish opened his trunk and showed Daniel something inside. Daniel smiled, shook his head and headed towards the house with Ish jogging behind him to catch up.

As the men arrived, Ed met them on the steps of the porch with a hearty handshake, and a slap on the back. We all made ourselves comfortable on the porch. Leon, Matty, and I sat in rocking chairs. Wayne sat on an aging porch swing; Daniel started to join him, but looked at the thin chains holding up the swing and thought better of it, and sat on the sturdy railing of the expansive front porch with Ed and Ish.

After twenty minutes of shooting the breeze, Ed gave us a tour of the house and the barn. The house was a large country brick farmhouse that I would guess had been built well before the Civil War. My guess was confirmed when Ed told us the house had been a stop on the Underground Railroad. He showed us his horses, and with just a hint of pride, his garden and orchard.

Ed had grilled hamburgers, chicken, and vegetables for us. He had also prepared homemade potato and macaroni salads. We stuffed ourselves with Ed's good cooking, washing down the meal with quarts of iced tea and lemonade. The men and I thanked Ed profusely for the meal and his hospitality. We took our drinks and poems to Ed's screened-in back porch and started our last session. I was getting ready to get the session started when Ed broke into a grin and looked over at Ish.

"Ish buddy, I gotta ask because I know the response is gonna be good. What did you show Daniel in your trunk?"

"I found me a dead fox on the side of the road."

"What do plan on doing with it, pray tell?" Wayne asked incredulously.

"Gonna make me one of them mountain man hats."

"Are you sure he was dead?" Matty asked.

"I poked him a couple times with my tire iron... he didn't move none."

"Do you know how to skin an animal, Ish?" Leon asked.

"No, but I'm sure I gots kinfolk somewhere that does."

"And what do you plan on doing with it in the meantime?" Wayne asked.

"Thought I'd stuff'im in my cousin Jasper's deep freeze. It'll scare the hell out of 'im when he finds it there!"

"I hope Jasper has a strong heart," Ed said. "I know a pretty good taxidermist, if you can't find knowledgeable kinfolk."

Ish had a puzzled look on his face.

"That's kind of ya, Ed, but I does my own taxes."

"Have you ever paid taxes, Ish?" Daniel asked.

"I'm lookin' into that."

Once again, the men got a kick out of Ish and his antics. It was hard to tell how much of his shtick was real or a put-on. Regardless, the levity was appreciated as we were about to start what I assumed would be a rather solemn meeting. After the laughter had died down, I cleared my throat and addressed the men.

"With pride and sadness I open up our last session. It has been an interesting adventure these past several months. I hope you have had as much healing and growth as I have had. Listening to your poems and your conversations have helped me a great deal in dealing with the loss of my father."

"Perhaps you should have written poems and taken photos along with us," Wayne said

"Well... actually... I have been."

"George, George, George, you've been holdin' out on us," Leon said, shaking his head.

"I wanted to keep my role as strictly the facilitator. This was about your healing... not mine."

225

"I respect that," Daniel said, "but you're part of our brotherhood. We would have welcomed reading and viewing your work."

"I realize that and really appreciate it... but, to be honest, I was intimidated by the work you all have produced... and this I must add. I've not only been inspired by your work, I've also been *influenced* by your work... and I mean *all* of you. I found myself writing poems with humor and surprise endings."

"Seriously?" Matty asked. "That's cool."

"Wayne and Matty have inspired me to write about my romantic mishaps. Leon's work has been an influence because many are written about the frustrations of teaching. Unfortunately, I do not possess his vivid imagination. I've written poems in the style of Daniel and Ed, where a working man's world is depicted with beauty and their technique of being very efficient with their words, reminiscent of one of my favorite writers, Raymond Carver."

"What about me boss?" Ish asked with a mock look of hurt on his face.

"Ish... from you... I've learned that one should write like one speaks. Write in your own voice. You, with Daniel's guidance, were able to paint a picture with your unique... perspective, and... your... colorful vernacular."

"I'm flattered, bla, bla, bla... and that's nice and all, but by not sharin', ya denied us, and by *us* I mean *me*, the chance to poke fun at ya."

"Sorry, Ish... but for the record... I played tennis in high school, so my backhand is almost as effective as Wayne's."

"Fair 'nuff."

"If we all stay in touch, and I hope we do, I'll share any work I do in the future... Now let's turn our attention back to our purpose for this whole adventure. I'd like you all to share your last poem and then if you are comfortable sharing the cause of your grief, you may do so. If not, just share the poem. Who would like to go first?"

"Normally a host lets his guests go first," Ed said. "But we'll make an exception this time and I'll go."

For Mary Pat

Imagine her eyes...
Loving, lucid, and light
Sky-blue and filled with laughter.
Eyes that sparkled,
Sparkled like distant stars.
Eyes that looked at you and
Listened as you spoke,
Held your words
Held them like rare gems
Careful not to drop a one
Eyes that could heal and give hope,
Loving lucid, and light.
Eyes of an artist that saw beauty
In this rough world and could capture
That beauty with strokes of a brush or pen.
Inviting eyes that welcomed,
Put you at ease,
Let you know you were a friend.
I miss those eyes
Loving, lucid, and light.

· · · · ·

"I've really enjoyed all of your previous work, Ed." Wayne said. "But that was different from your other poems. It's beautiful. I assume she was someone you loved very deeply."

"Very much, but I didn't realize it until she was gone."

"Was she your wife?" Leon asked.

"No, she was my partner."

"I thought only gay folks had partners," Ish said confused.

"She was not a romantic partner; she was my partner on the police force... for over twelve years. She died three years ago."

"Did she die in the line of duty?" Matty asked.

"No... she took her own life. She had a great deal going on in her life, a recent divorce and some health issues. I would assume the stress of the job was also a factor. The grief I felt... and the guilt I carried with me for not... being more aware, was destructive. I was pissed at the world; I started abusing alcohol, made poor choices on the job. I was advised to retire before I was let go. It ultimately cost me my own marriage, which brought me down even deeper."

We were all very silent as we looked at the sadness in Ed's eyes. Daniel broke the silence.

"I'm sorry you went through all that, my friend. I can imagine that was, and still is, painful for you."

"It's getting better. Time has helped, as well as the serenity of living and working here. And honestly, George, I've felt even better after starting this writing project. The writing as well as the comradery have been healing."

"Amen," Leon said with his head bowed and his hand raised to the sky.

"Good to hear," I said. "Dad would be pleased to know you are healing and that we are a part of it. Is there anything else you would like to talk about?"

"I want to add that I have been talking to my ex-wife again. There is a chance we might be able to patch things up. She is willing to see me again; no promises, but it's a start."

"Good luck with that," I said. "Thanks for sharing your story. I know these things aren't easy to talk about."

"I'll go next," Wayne said.

When Do I Think of You?

You ask me
   when do I think of you.
I think of you when
   I'm driving and that song
comes on the radio,
   You know the one.
I think of you when
   extraordinary clouds roll in.
My quirky fascination
   was contagious.
I apologize for that.
   I think of you when
I pass that spot
   where we lunch
that warm June day.
   I joked about carving
our initials into
   that picnic table.
Now, regretting
   that I didn't.
I think of you
   At night

when I gaze at stars
   and realize
they're shining
   on you as well.
When do I think of you?
   Honestly, too often.
The abstract thinking that
   you liked about me,
is now clouded, obscured

I could ask,
   When do you think of me?
But, I won't ask
   for fear that you
would hesitate,
   tell a lie.
A disappointment
   that would be,
frankly,
   too much to bear.

• • • • •

"That started out so romantic and then…" Leon trailed off, not finishing the sentence.

"Kind of like all of my relationships. My grief pales in comparison to what Ed went through, and probably the rest of you as well."

"It's not a contest, buddy," Leon said. "Loss is loss."

"My grief is my divorce from my wife. I was so in love with her, but she was abusive. Mentally not physically. Can you guess where she ended up?"

"Buried in your crawl space?" Ish asked.

"No, but the thought crossed my mind. She left me for my best friend. To say I have trust issues now is an understatement. I keep finding myself in abusive relationships like that. I try too much to please, and I end up being taken advantage of. It's frustrating and very lonely."

"I'm the last guy to give relationship advice," Daniel said. "But I would think the fact that you are aware of your tendency to be walked on, is a start. We've witnessed your ability to stand up for yourself."

"I hear that. He can stand up for hisself while he's *sittin'*!" Ish said emphatically.

"It sounds like your current relationship is similar to that of your marriage," Ed said. "Would that be accurate?"

Before Wayne could answer, Ish chimed in with his words of wisdom.

"Dump her ass."

"I did, thank you very much, two weeks ago."

"There you go," Leon said enthusiastically. "An opportunity to turn things around."

"Is your sister still available, Ish?" Matty asked with a straight face.

"Uh, I believe it's someone else's turn to share," Wayne said hurriedly.

"Sounds good," I said. "Thanks, Wayne. I really enjoyed your poem. Again, I know the story behind it was not easy to share. We appreciate your honesty. Who's next?"

"I'll go," Matty offered. "No picture for this one… even though it's about a picture. You need to use your imagination to make this one work."

Ode to a Picture of My Father

It's there in the picture.
The rusty hair and mustache.
The casual, easy lean, slight tilt of the head,
A wry smile.
Thumbs hooked in jean pockets.
Cool personified.
Yet, what the picture belies.
Hiding behind that contentment.
A splintered past,
Abandonment, rejection, loneliness, a longing for roots, stability.
An all too familiar list.
Not a single witness to help answer all those questions.
Intelligence, vivid recollections, a blessing and a curse.
Humor, dry wit, helped to mask the pain.
Tried your damnedest to not wallow in self-pity.
How difficult that must have been.
So you threw yourself into your passions.
Those beautiful distractions.
Boxing, Picasso, the smoky rhythms of a jazz drum,
Consuming- no *devouring*- the written word.
And best of all, a country girl with raven hair.
The one who had faith in you, saved you.
But you couldn't shake that dark companion.
That followed those before you... and some after.
Did you pass on that melancholy and the broken dreams?
I think we know the answer.

•   •   •   •   •

"Wow," Leon whispered. "Dark and beautiful."

"I love it," Wayne said, "but it made me tremendously sad... you okay, George?"

The poem had hit me pretty hard.

"Yeah, sorry," I said with a catch in my throat. "I'm sorry for your loss, Matty. Great poem- made me think of my own dad. I miss him a great deal."

"I think you probably hit a nerve with most of us," Daniel said. "I, for one, thought about the complicated relationship I had with my old man. Had to learn to love him... and forgive him."

"Your dad sounded like an interesting and perplexing man, Matty," Ed said. "How long has he been gone?"

"He's been gone about two years. He was incredibly smart and extremely funny. He amazed us every day. The toughest part has been the fact there was so much about him that was a mystery to us. He really struggled, like many men, with expressing his emotions. I don't think it was ever modeled for him. It was foreign territory."

"Unfortunately," Ed said sadly, "I can relate to that."

"I would guess many of us can," Daniel murmured.

Matty took a deep breath and blew it out before he spoke.

"As a kid I wanted to know how he felt about me. There were times I could sense he was frustrated with me, but I wouldn't know why. There were times I think he was proud of me but he didn't really say it. I knew his past was rough and I wanted to be understanding. At the time I was too young to know what to do."

Ed reached over with his big calloused hand and gently patted Matty on the back.

"The best thing you could have done was to be a good son, which I'm sure you were."

"I made mistakes, but I tried. I worry that his depression was partly in his genes... and now in my genes."

"But the difference is, you have the knowledge, the tools, to handle it," Daniel said. "He would be proud of the man you've turned into."

"Thanks. I appreciate that. You all have helped fill the void... been role models for me."

We were all pleased and perhaps a little embarrassed by the praise. Leon, on cue, lightened the mood.

"Congratulations, Ish! You've become a father!"

"Well now, 'em are words I was hopin' never to hear. But, as ya'll knows,I'm not one to shirk his responsibilities. I am willin' ta help raise ya best I can. Teach ya all the manly things a fella needs to know."

In spite of the somber mood, I knew the men were going to have a field day with this.

"Like how to shoot pool and to gamble?" Leon asked.

"How to deliver a pizza in less than thirty minutes," Wayne added.

"How to hotwire a car and do your own dental work," Daniel said.

"Sure, sure," Ish said nodding his head. "And other important stuff, like the birds and the bees."

"Geez, Ish!" Leon exclaimed, "The guy's twenty-one years old!"

"Well his daddy mighta passed on before the big speech."

"I would pay good money to sit in on that conversation," Daniel said with a grin.

"That all sounds good, Ish," Matty said. "I'll let ya know."

"I'm here for ya... Son."

"Okay, Ish," Leon said. "I think the kid's been through a great deal; we don't want to traumatize him anymore. I'll save the kid and go next if that's okay with everyone? I need to start off by saying; this was the most difficult thing I've ever written."

Dreams, Be Done With Me

There was a time when I invited dreams.
Those vivid adventures of endless possibilities,
quirky twists, nonsensical turns, and abrupt stops.
Clicking by at breakneck speed like an art film.

Wake with a curious smile.
What in the hell was the meaning of that one?
Those ominous premonitions beyond interpretation,
or the erotic followed by the guilt of rewinding.

But, that was before we lost him.
Now the dreams are uninvited guests, like storm troopers in black boots.
Cursed to relive that night, a haunting, repeating loop.

Doorbell rings at three a.m.
Walk past his room and see the empty bed.
Heart racing, I rush down the stairs.
The solemn stranger, hat in hand, delivers the grim news.

Then, the unbearable cruelty, worse, if possible, than the truth.
The constant, euphoric dreams that it was all a mistake.
Upon waking the devastating realization that it was not
Deep sorrow once more relived.

Damn you, dreams.
I beg you, be done with me.

•   •   •   •   •

The only sound that could be heard were the birds in the country air beyond the porch.

"Before anyone says anything," Leon said quietly, his voice catching. "Let me explain what happened. This will keep you from holding back on questions you might want to ask, but feel uncomfortable asking.

I lost my oldest son in a car accident 18 months ago. I'd rather not go over the details. I relived that night in my dreams many times, and then I had dreams where he was alive, telling me it was all a mistake. Then I would wake up, and realize he was still gone... The depth of my sorrow was almost unbearable. You see, I had lost my wife to cancer ten years ago. I was not sure if I had the strength to deal with another loss.

My kids were what saved me. They were hurting as much as I was, yet they were worried about me, and we did the best to comfort each other. I knew I had to keep it together; I still had three kids who needed me. It's tough... but we're makin' it."

Everyone was moved in his own way. I could not hold back the tears so I just let them flow. From the sniffing I could hear I think some of the others were doing the same. I kept my head down, staring at a spot on the floor. We were silent for a time before Ed broke the silence.

"I think I can speak for everyone, Leon. We are so sorry for the loss of your son... and your wife. I can only begin to imagine what you have been through. I never would have guessed the pain you've endured... you have to be the most upbeat person I've ever met."

"Thanks, I should have been an actor," Leon said with a sad chuckle. "But seriously, I've always been a positive person, and humor is in my nature, but I hide behind it sometimes... sound familiar, Matty? Besides the strength of my family, the staff at my school- especially my friend Stan- has been incredible... and I have to agree with the others, George. The writing and the camaraderie have been therapeutic... and a hell of a great distraction."

"Amen," Ish whispered reverently.

"Again, I know these losses are not easy to talk about," I said, "and I hope the pain we are reliving will help us to have... perhaps not closure, but to help us towards healing."

"Grievin' sucks," Ish said, again in a whisper.

"I've heard this quote numerous times," Ed said. "Given the choice between grieving and nothing, I'll take grieving."

"The dude who said that sucks," Ish said.

"Faulkner," Daniel said.

"Faulkner sucks," Wayne said, uncharacteristically. This brought out a smile or a chuckle from every man.

"Grief is part of the human condition," Leon said. "I get that, but I've had my full share and I'm ready to live and focus on all the good I have going on. I'll still grieve but I'm not going to let it consume me."

"Well gentleman, I was on the fence about sharing tonight, but you all have inspired me," Daniel said.

East of Anywhere

Am I my brother's keeper?
Cain's reply to God,
a deflection to hide his heinous crime.

Am I my brother's keeper?
A rhetorical question,
meaning we have a responsibility
to take care of our fellow man.

Am I my brother's keeper?
a haunting reminder
of falling short,
failing to keep a promise.

Sometimes the sacrifice you make
has an unintended consequence.
Blood cries out from the ground
as you wander the earth.
Your curse, your mark, the question;
Was I my brother's keeper?

• • • • •

"Story of Cain and Abel, book of Genesis," Ish said with a far off look in his eyes.

"You know your Old Testament," Daniel said quietly.

"Granny sat in a rocker and read to us from the Good Book every damn day when I was a kid. It was torture... but, some of it stuck."

"Did you lose a brother, Daniel?

"His name was Paul, but we called him Sonny. I tried like hell to help him... keep him out of trouble. I bailed him out, loaned him money... knowing I'd never be repaid. Helped him find work, let him crash on my couch. Figuratively and literally gave him the shirt off my back. He was starting to get his act together, but, occasionally, he would still hang out with the wrong crowd. I, also, do not want to go into details, but Sonny was shot and killed because he was in the wrong place at the wrong time. He wasn't the intended target; he was collateral damage."

"Sounds like you are not only grieving but struggling with guilt as well," Leon said.

"Unfortunately, grief and guilt often go hand in hand. I've subconsciously punished myself by drifting from city to city, always settling on the east side of town."

"East of Eden, in the land of Nod," Ish said reverently.

"I think many of us have beaten ourselves up over our losses," Ed said. "Did they ever catch the shooter or shooters?"

"The police didn't... but two of my brothers did."

"Any guilt tied to that?"

"Guilt that they took matters into their own hands? ... No. Guilt that I didn't help? ... a little bit... My brothers didn't want me involved so they kept me out of the loop. I don't have a criminal record, and they wanted to keep it that way. They let the guys live... which honestly, surprised me. They called the police and told them where to find them. The detective working the case was probably relieved and pissed off at the same time. I assume he found them in pretty rough shape."

"I hope your pain is starting to subside," Leon said.

"It has. As a matter of fact, I'm done drifting... for a while at least. I like it here."

"I'm really glad to hear that, Daniel," I said. "I hope you don't mind, and I do not mean to overstep my bounds, but I talked to some connections my mother has in the Art History Department. There might be an opening for a grad assistant if you are interested."

All eyes went from me to Daniel. I really hope I did the right thing. Perhaps this wasn't the best time to bring it up. He looked at me for a long time before he spoke.

"So this is where I usually get pissed and ask you to stay out of my business, or politely turn you down, or say, 'I'll think about it'... and never get back to you... but, I'll do none of those things... I'm interested... and I really appreciate you looking into that for me."

The wave of relief and elation I felt was palpable. I didn't realize I was holding my breath until I let out a large exhale that made everyone chuckle.

"Great! When we are done tonight I'll tell you who you need to contact... and thanks for not kicking my ass for getting in your business."

"C'mon, George," Daniel said with a look of mock hurt, his smile dissolving. "You know me better than that by now. Wayne's the one you gotta watch out for."

"That's right," Wayne said with mock attitude. "And if any of you bitches forget that, I'll backhand your punk-ass!"

The porch erupted with laughter... even Ish found it funny. The mood had been dark due to the nature of our poems and the conversations that followed. The laughter was a little forced but welcomed.

"Okay, Ish," I said. "You will be the last one to share tonight."

"Before I present mine I'd like to share somethin' with y'all. Daniel seems to think the reason I struggle with readin' and writin' is 'cause I might have somethin' called dicklessia."

"*Dyslexia*," Daniel corrected with a laugh.

"I would assume he suffers from both," Wayne said straight-faced.

"It's just a feeling I have based on working with him," Daniel said. "Would we be able to get him tested?"

"I would be glad to look into that," I said. "If you want that, Ish."

"Let me do it, George," Leon said. "I can get him tested and get him some help if he needs it. Would you be willing to get tested Ish?"

"Will they poke me with needles?"

"No. Not unless you want them to."

"Sign me up."

"Years ago I pulled over a guy for doing 53 in a 35," Ed said. "He apologizes and says he's got dyslexia. I let him go with a warning."

"Felt sorry for him?" Matty asked.

"No, I assume he was lyin'. I let him go for being creative."

"I'm gonna remember that one," Ish said. "Daniel was busy this week, so I had that cute library lady help me out. Here's my poem."

Caged

I kept you caged up,
and you knew why.
I had to protect you from those cool cats,
prowlin' the 'hood, wantin' a piece.
In the dark
I could sense your restlessness, your fear.
Holding you, stroking your hair,
did little to calm your hammering heart.
You'd listen to my quiet whispers,
but they were pointless,
wasted words, a foreign language.
But I got careless, let you slip away,
out the door into that devouring black night.
I might not ever hold you again, but Alice,
this you must know,
you were more than just a hamster,
you were the best fuzzy little friend a guy could own.
Seriously,
I mean it.

•   •   •   •   •

There was a full minute of complete silence.

"Sweet Jesus," Leon mumbled.

"Unbelievable," Matty said softly while looking at the ground.

I knew I had to say something but I really didn't know what to say, how to handle it. I was in shock. I cleared my throat and the group turned and looked at me.

"I'm at a loss..."

"I know, I know. I was real... sad... and stuff," Ish said, eyes closed, massaging his temples with his fingertips.

"You got guys pouring their hearts out over lost loved ones, and your grief is over a hamster? Are you serious?" Daniel growled.

"Like I said, I was real sad..."

"... and *stuff*. Whatever that means." Daniel said, his frustration rising.

"You have to admit, Ish, this seems a little far-fetched..." Ed said.

"Even coming from you," Wayne added.

"Okay, okay... everyone just get off my ass! I wasn't... I didn't... really... have any grief."

"Did you do it for the money?" Daniel asked, the anger smoldering.

"That's what caught my eye when I saw the flier... but..."

"This had better be good, brother," Leon said glaring at him.

"I was lonely," Ish said in a meek whisper.

"And?" Leon pushed.

Ish sat up straight and looked around the room. He let out a long sigh, threw up his hands and shrugged his shoulders.

"That's it. That's all I got."

"You've talked about having friends," Leon said.

"My friends are bigger jerks than I am," Ish said shaking his head.

"It's hard to believe, but it's true... I've met them," Daniel said, the anger leaving his voice.

"Loneliness is painful... I know," Wayne said softly.

"What did you tell my dad when he interviewed you? Did you lie to him?" I asked.

"I told him I was grievin' over the loss of my close friend Alice. I failed to mention Alice was a hamster."

"He bought your story? Dad was pretty astute."

"That's the funny thing. I had a feelin' he knew I was stretchin' the truth."
I tossed around what he said in my mind before I spoke.

"He knew you needed this group... That it would be good for you."

"Maybe he wanted to add a little color to the group," Ed said.

"Leon's the one with color. I'm 'bout as white as they come. I keep tellin' y'all that." Ish said defiantly.

"With the exception of your neck," Daniel said the anger returning a bit. "It's as *red* as they come."

"I meant, he thought you would make the group interesting... and you have," Ed clarified.

"Amen," Wayne added.

"I'm sorry I was deceitful," Ish said. "I like y'all and consider ya my friends. I'm glad I'm in the group, but how I went about gettin' in... was dead wrong."

"It's alright, Ish," Leon said. "You've taught us patience and tolerance."

"Thank ya... I think. The library lady helped we with this poem, cleaned 'er up pretty good. I tried to thank 'er, but she said it was okay, that I was a 'Spiritual test' for her. Whatever that means."

"Well it all worked out," I said. "Ish was meant to be here."

"We all were," Ed said with a grin.

"I agree," I said. "Myself included. As you all know, I'm not an expert on grief, or any kind of counseling for that matter. I do know that dad wasn't a proponent of Kubler-Ross's five stages of grief."

"Neither was she in the later years of her life," Daniel said. "I read she regretted coming up with those."

I was relieved someone knew what I was talking about. Kubler-Ross isn't in everyone's wheelhouse.

"Dad, and I'm sure many, many others, believed that a person proceeded through grief at their own pace and that people all grieve differently. If it were like stair steps, you might go up and down not just straight up towards acceptance. A person could be angry for a time, not be angry, and then be angry again. I think it would be difficult to tell people that they are grieving the wrong way. You feel what you feel. We might not ever accept the loss we have experienced, but we cope and we continue to live and thrive the best we can."

"Having someone listen to you and support you is crucial," Ed said. "At least it was for me."

"To paraphrase a wise man," Leon said. "'A person needs their mates.'"

"Freud? Jung?" Matty guessed.

"I believe it was Paul Hogan in the movie *Crocodile Dundee*," Daniel said.

"Correct, as usual," Leon said. "Dundee is listening to an explanation about a woman who went to see a shrink to unload her problems. Dundee says, 'Hasn't she got any mates?' He goes on to explain that where he is from, if you have a problem you tell a friend and get it out in the open; then the problem goes away."

"It's not always that simple," I said, "but there's a lot of truth to that."

"For me, I feel the writing, the photography, the camaraderie, *all* have been beneficial," Ed said. "I would not have done anything different. Thank you, George."

"Thanks, but I've done very little. You guys were the engine that ran this thing and my dad was the one who started it."

"I think the poems revealed stuff about us before we knew it ourselves, even the humorous ones," Daniel said. "Like the score for an opera, the orchestra knows or reveals the truth before the actors do."

"This might be a good time to share a poem I wrote," I said.

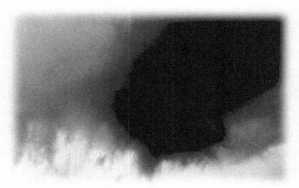

Goodbyes

Goodbyes can roll in like a summer storm,
unexpected, quick, and sometimes devastating.
Goodbyes can be thieves, stealing what's precious.
Goodbyes can be sutures, closing wounds, helping us heal.
So this is my goodbye, and I struggle to find the right words...
Words I want to stack in neat rows, like bricks.
I'll fill those gaps of awkward silence
with a mortar of mindless small-talk.

    I need to remember that goodbyes can be a building, and depending on
the intention, a wall, a barrier that   separates.

    or a foundation, a solid place to build upon.

•   •   •   •   •

"That was really cool, George," Matty said. "You've got skills with words and a camera. But, honestly, I don't want to say goodbye, I don't want to stop. After we are done, I'm going to keep writing and taking pictures. I also hope I can maintain the friendships I've gained."

"Who says we have to stop?" Leon said. "Can't we keep meeting, let's say once a month or so? If you don't have anything to share, you come anyway to hang out."

"I'm in," Ed said. "We can meet here if you'd like."

"Count me in as well," Wayne said. "Ish?"

"Yep."

"I'm in," Daniel said. "George, of course I insist, I mean *we* insist, that you be a part of this as well."

"It would be an honor."

"But, now that we know you have talent," Daniel continued, "you have to write and take pictures as well; it's only fair, Brother."

"You're right; it's only fair," I said. "Now I'll feel like I'm part of the group instead of an observer."

"Did you bring a guitar college boy?" Ish asked. "I think we's about to break inta a round of Kumbaya."

"Don't worry, Ish," I said. "I'm not going to get mushy on ya."

"I hate to break up this party," Ed said, "but I got a farrier coming early in the morning."

Ish threw his hands up in the air in mock surrender. "Whoa now, I didn't know ya swung that way, Ed... But, who am I to judge, to each his own."

"A farrier puts shoes on a horse," Leon said laughing.

"I knew that."

"Hey guys, I know this a strange thought," Matty said. "But if what we just went through for the past ten weeks was a novel."

"That would be one strange book," Ed said.

"Oh I agree. I was just wondering who would be the protagonist?" Matty asked with a grin.

"I think that would have to be George," Leon said.

"Can't we all be the protagonists?" I asked.

"Just like a teacher; everybody gets his fair share," Ed said with a grin.

"Many experts would argue a story should have only one protagonist," Daniel said.

"I decline; I'm too busy," Ed said.

"I have a good idea who would be the antagonist," Daniel said.

All eyes fixed on Ish.

"I ain't no antagonist!" Ish snarled, "I'm a Baptist!"

The rest of us burst into laughter. Although he wasn't sure why, Ish joined in. It felt good.

So that's how it all went down. Did the experiment work? I think so. To what extent would be difficult to measure, and might not matter all that much. It's obvious that the act of, and the art of, creating is powerful. Combine that with a sense of community and camaraderie and great things can happen. So to paraphrase Uncle Walt, 'The powerful play goes on... and *we* may contribute a verse.'

Acknowledgments

It takes a village to write a book. These are my village people.

First and foremost, my family and friends who believed in me and the project from the start. The feedback you gave, and at times didn't give, speak volumes.

To Black Rose Writing for your interest, help, promotion, and for making this project possible for others to see on a larger stage.

Thanks to Diane Haddad for editing. You caught things I would never have seen. Your sharp eye and tactful suggestions made editing fun.

To Sally Brink for help with editing and the workings of law enforcement.

Margaret Evans, LPC, for your advice and guidance on how group counseling works. Thank you for sharing your expertise, your positivity, your own great writing, photography and your spirit.

Thanks to my unpaid models: Zeke Thorpe, Sam Thorpe, Alexa Thorpe, Eli Thorpe, Beth Thorpe, Kristin Konopka, Christian Hipp, Shawn Sullivan, and Kim Murray's 7-Eleven Big Gulp cup.

The staff at Hilliard City Schools for all the encouragement and excitement. I have the best job in the world!

Finally, to Tony Beccaccio. You have pushed me to write and keep writing for decades. I never would have considered publishing had you not been so persistent. Our great friend and fellow writer, Dr. Terry Webb, is looking down from heaven with that ever-present smile.

Thank you so much for reading one of our **Humor** novels.
If you enjoyed our book, please check out our recommended title for your
next great read!

Parrot Talk by David B. Seaburn

"...a story of abandonment, addiction, finding oneself—all mixed in with
tear-jerking chapters next to laugh-out-loud chapters." *—Tiff & Rich*

View other Black Rose Writing titles at www.blackrosewriting.com/books

and use promo code **PRINT** to receive a **20% discount** when purchasing.